Blackwater Falls:
Plan B

Shannon West and Susan E Scott

Plan B

Copyright © 2014

Published by Dark Hollows Press

About the eBook You Have Purchased

All rights reserved. Without reserving the rights under copyright, reserved above, no part of this publication may be reproduced, stored in or introduced into a retrieval system, or transmitted in any form, or any other means (electronic, mechanical, photocopying, recording or otherwise) without the prior written permission of the copyright owner and the above publisher of this book. Distribution of this e-book, in whole or in part, is forbidden. Such action is illegal and in violation of the U.S. Copyright Law.

Dark Hollows Press, LLC

P.O. Box 343, Silver Creek GA 30173

Plan B

Copyright © 2014

Authors: Shannon West and Susan E Scott

ISBN 10: 1499594631
ISBN 13: 978-1499594638
Original E-book Publication Date: December 2013
Original Print Publication: May 2014
All cover art and logo copyright © 2014 by Dark Hollows Press

ALL RIGHTS RESERVED: This literary work may not be reproduced or transmitted in any form or by any means, including electronic or photographic reproduction, in whole or in part, without express written permission.
All characters and events in this book are fictitious. Any resemblance to actual persons living or dead is strictly coincidental.

Chapter One

Some things in Travis's life hadn't always gone exactly to plan. The cards hadn't fallen the right way, the lottery numbers had been just a few off, and the car had almost been in the safety of the driveway when the blue lights appeared in the rearview mirror. When that happened, there was only one thing to do—fall back on Plan B. Except that on this particular Saturday night, Travis Sutherland didn't have much of a plan of any kind, "B" or otherwise.

He had partied way too much earlier in the evening, with a lot of alcohol and maybe a few too many hits off the bong that was being passed around, and he had that nice floaty feeling like he was flying along just above the road. He was still high, but not too bad, and he knew he could make it home if he took it nice and slow. His car weaving a bit, he was trying to keep it between the ditches. There was little traffic on this old back road so he was good. He was better than good. He was in a groove and feeling no pain.

It was then he noticed a flash in the rearview mirror and looked up to see the blue lights. Groaning, he pulled carefully over to the side of the road and waited to see who would get out of the vehicle. Fuck. Of course, it had to be Hawke, his cousin and the local sheriff. Things were definitely not looking up.

Plan B

For most people, having one of your relatives pull you over after a bit too much to drink would be a good thing—unfortunately, Travis wasn't one of those people. And Hawke wasn't one of those kinds of relatives. Hawke was a hard-ass and would cut him absolutely no slack. The fact that he and Travis's older brother, Spencer, were best friends didn't bode well either. He'd be lucky not to wind up under the jail.

He watched his cousin warily in the side mirror as he got out of the vehicle and sauntered up to the driver's door of the car, oozing cop attitude. Shining a flashlight in his eyes, Hawke held it there for a moment before sweeping it over the interior of the car. "Where you headed, Travis?"

Trying for a pleasant voice, Travis replied, "Just on my way home, Hawke. Almost in the driveway."

"You been smoking a little weed, Travis?"

"Well, hell no. What would make you think that?"

"For one thing, you reek of it, though it's kind of hard to tell, since you also smell like a damn brewery. Get out of the car, Travis."

"What for?"

"Because I'm asking you to."

"Ah, damn, Hawke, please. Just let me go home. I'm almost there."

"Can't do it. What if you got fifty feet down the road, ran off in a ditch and flipped your vehicle? Or worse yet, hit some other driver on the way home? What's your family going to say knowing I let you drive in this condition?"

"Oh, for God's sake, Hawke. Don't you think that's a little bit dramatic?"

"No, I don't. Not in the condition you're in—I don't even know how you're still conscious. Now get your ass out of the damn car."

Realizing that he couldn't win this argument, Travis opened the door and wearily stumbled out of the front seat, nearly face-planting when his feet hit the ground. Hawke grabbed his arm to steady him, heroically refraining from saying anything else, though Travis figured it must have cost him dearly.

Travis's mama was going to have his ass for this, not to mention having to listen to his dad and Spencer, but his mama was a force to be reckoned with. One of the clan females, Emma Sutherland, was known both for her prodigiously bad temper, even worse than the norm for clan females, and her ability to talk so long and so loud that any would-be opponent just gave up. Although Travis was her youngest son and her pride and joy, she would ream his ass for this one.

All this was making Travis seriously lose his buzz, and he wanted to go home, get in his own bed, and block out everything for a few hours. His head was beginning to pound, and he thought there was a distinct possibility he might throw up on Hawke's shoes. He stayed where Hawke put him, next to the back bumper. Hawke's flashlight moved away to sweep over the interior of his car.

Plan B

If only Holden had let him stay at his place tonight this wouldn't have happened. He rubbed a hand over his face, silently cursing Holden MacKay and what seemed to be his increasing lack of interest in Travis—the main reason Travis had tied one on in the first damn place.

He and Holden had hung out and partied together for the past year or so, had even shared some pretty hot make-out sessions, but that was all. Holden seemed to want to keep him as little more than a friend.

Travis knew he was good-looking. No sense lying about it. He'd been voted Best Looking Senior Superlative in high school, along with being the Homecoming King and the Prom King in both his junior and senior years. He wasn't particularly conceited about it—it was an accident of birth after all. But still, he couldn't understand why Holden didn't seem to want to have sex with him. It wasn't like Travis hadn't offered often enough.

Male or female didn't much matter to the clan members, who were remarkably without prejudices about sexuality, considering the fact that they'd always lived in the Bible Belt south where it mattered quite a bit to most folks. It was a fact that many of the clan were just as happy with a same sex partner as not, and sexual preference was entirely left up to the individual. In that respect, at least, they were an open-minded society, but there was one thing that clan members couldn't seem to do very well, and that was to be mated to each other.

Casual sex was okay, and frequent, really, with so many young, attractive clan members running wild on the dark of the moon, but a true mating between clan members was rare and extremely difficult to pull off. The fact was that they were all too damn dominant and aggressive to ever co-exist peacefully together. There had been instances, of course, over the years when two clan members got a mating call for each other, but the situations never ended well and usually not without bloodshed.

Most clan members picked themselves out a nice, uncomplicated human, who usually fell completely under their spell, seeing as how clan members were almost always quite attractive. Sometimes there was even a mating instinct for a human, like with Hawke and his mate, Jace. It used to be more common, but over the years the clan blood had become watered down by the constant infusion of human DNA. Now mating calls were becoming increasingly rare.

It was said that in times past, clan members mated regularly together, but not anymore. At some point in the not too distant past, clan women had become stronger and more domineering, forcing clan males to look elsewhere for their mates. Matings between two clan males however, was almost unheard of. Sex between them might be possible, but they'd never be able to live together for long without one of them killing or seriously injuring the other in a bid for control.

Plan B

In the meantime, there was nothing wrong with fooling around and experimenting, like Travis wanted to do with the gorgeous Holden, but Holden was still holding him at arm's length, even after a year.

Holden was older, more his brother Spencer's age, and the unacknowledged head of the MacKay clan. The MacKays, like the Sutherlands, had lived in the Alabama mountains for hundreds of years, and had originally come over from Scotland around the same time as the Sutherlands.

That didn't mean the two clans were friendly, though, and his relationship with Holden was very much a sore spot with his family. There had been bad blood between the Sutherlands and the MacKays since the great clan wars in Scotland around the fourteenth century. The feud first came to a head then, when a Sutherland murdered the head of the MacKay clan in his own bed. Things had gone downhill from there.

"Sit over in my car, Hotshot, while I call a wrecker." Hawke jerked his head toward the patrol car and Travis decided to give it one last try.

"A wrecker? Please, Hawke, it's not but a mile or two up the road to the house! Hell, just park my car on the side of the road and I'll walk. Please?"

"No."

"Damn it, Hawke, can't you call Spencer to come pick up my car?"

"I could, but I won't. If your mama and daddy have to pay for a wrecker, maybe they'll lay the law down on you before I have to. This kind of shit is going to get you killed, boy, and I, for one, don't have any desire to go to your damn funeral. Now sit in my car and shut the hell up. Consider yourself damn lucky I'm not taking you to jail—and I would be if the dark moon wasn't tomorrow night."

Travis decided maybe he better do as he was told, because Hawke didn't seem to be in the best of moods tonight. As usual on the night before the dark of the moon, everybody was edgy and feeling the strain. Maybe that had been the cause of Holden's rudeness earlier, when Travis had tried to get him to take him upstairs to bed. Like the Sutherlands, the MacKays had the curse.

"Go home, Travis, and sleep it off," Holden had said. "I've already had one visit from your family this week, and I have no desire for another one."

"My family came to see you! What?" Travis had cried out, incensed and embarrassed. He knew it had to be Spencer, and it infuriated him that his brother would involve himself in his relationship with Holden. Travis was twenty-one years old and a grown man—he didn't need anybody's interference. "They have no say in what I do or don't do!"

"Well, they seem to think they do. They told me to leave you alone. Not only that, but Spencer and Hawke were over here making threats about me selling alcohol in the bar to underage boys from Blackwater Falls." He turned an angry face toward Travis. "You told me all those boys were legal, Travis."

"They are! Well, most of them are, anyway. One or two of them might be only nineteen…"

"Damn it, Travis!" He pushed him away then when Travis tried to hug him, and turned him and his friends out, telling them all to go home.

Since Travis and Holden were both shifters, even though they were from different clans, they had no future together and they knew it. He realized that the other man didn't love him, and Travis didn't love Holden either, really, but, it still hurt to be dismissed like that. If Holden wasn't so hot and Travis didn't need to get laid so damn bad, he'd give some thought to breaking it off with him. As it was, he was afraid that Holden would soon be putting *him* on the road.

Travis was brought out of this reverie by Hawke's voice. "Okay, Travis. I'll call the garage to come tow your car to the house, and then I'll drive you home."

Knowing that it was useless to try to talk Hawke out of it, and grateful that he wasn't being taken to jail, Travis put his head back on the headrest of the passenger seat in Hawke's vehicle. "Okay, fine then. Jesus, stop dragging it out. Let's just go."

"Hold your damn horses. Sit over there and shut up, or I'll put you in cuffs and throw your ass in the back. We have to wait on the tow truck. I'm calling MacKay's now." Travis folded his arms and narrowed his eyes. He knew better than to say anything more when Hawke was looking at him like that, but it didn't mean he didn't want to. It damn near choked him to death to sit there and not tell Hawke exactly what he thought of him and his highhanded ways.

He honestly didn't know how Jace, Hawke's new mate, could stand him. Jace was close to Travis's age and seemed pretty cool, but Hawke had always been an arrogant, opinionated asshole. Hawke was like a big brother to him in a lot of ways, but still, at times like these, he pissed Travis off.

Travis felt like he'd been sitting in Hawke's vehicle for hours, but it had probably only been about fifteen minutes before he heard the tow truck coming down the road. When it stopped in front of his car and the driver jumped out, Travis wanted to slide down in the seat out of sight. *Camron MacKay. Of all people, why him?*

Travis had gone to high school with Camron, but he doubted that Camron would remember him. Travis was two years younger, and Camron had been a big football star and absolutely the best-looking male in his class or any other as far as Travis was concerned. Travis had a huge crush on Camron his sophomore year in high school and still felt fidgety every time he saw him. The only problem was that Camron was rather aggressively straight, which was odd for a clan male, and he had never shown the slightest interest in Travis one way or the other.

Travis heard Hawke talking to Camron, but couldn't make out what he was saying. Then, Camron started past the police vehicle, stopping to look in and smile at Travis.

"Hey, Travis, got yourself in a little trouble again, huh? As soon as I can get this hooked up, I'll tow it to your house. It won't take but a minute."

Plan B

"Okay. Thanks, Camron." Camron nodded and looked back at the tow truck behind him. Travis's gaze followed his, and he flushed when he saw Jenny Calhoun sitting up in the front seat, waiting for Camron. Her Barbie doll blonde hair was being twirled around a finger as she gazed out the window and when she saw Camron looking at her, she gave him a little wave.

Camron must have been on a date with Jenny when Hawke called. Camron was the owner of MacKay's Garage, and usually the one on call after hours. He was also one of Holden's cousins, not that they got along at all. Holden was of the opinion that the feud between the Sutherlands and the MacKay's was still alive and well, while Camron and most of the other younger members of the MacKay clan thought of it as ancient history. There was no doubt in most people's minds, though, that the curse came directly from the Sutherlands.

It seemed that back in the day, several of the Sutherland women were kidnapped, raped and held captive by the MacKays, and it brought the curse into their own family. The curse was an interesting Sutherland ability to shift into a big mountain lion on the dark of the moon. It must have freaked the hell out of the MacKays when they discovered what their wives became during the three nights of the dark of the moon, but by that time, it must have already been too late. The notorious clan charm had taken its toll on the MacKay men and they refused to give their wives up.

They still blamed the Sutherlands, of course, but their wives must have been something pretty special, because they protected them in a time when most people would have just burned them at the stake and been done with it. That was the beginning of the love/hate relationship between the two families. Of course, a great deal of all this so-called history was just legend and myth, but the seemingly impossible fact remained that his family, along with the MacKays weren't exactly human, and probably never had been.

Pretty little Jenny Calhoun was human and had been in Travis's high school class. Like most of the people they went to school with, the humans had no idea about the clan secrets. Only the humans who were chosen as mates by the clan ever had any idea about their true nature.

Camron, like most clan males, was obviously avoiding the clan females, and had picked out this little human for himself. Travis didn't know why that should cause him a little twinge that felt suspiciously like jealousy, but it did. Hell, it wasn't like Camron would ever have any interest in him anyway.

He put his head back on the seat again and tried not to think about his mama's reaction when Hawke brought him home. Please God, let her be asleep and not wake up until Hawke was already gone. If she came out on the porch and raised hell with Hawke, he might haul Travis to jail anyway just out of spite. His mama had practically helped raise Hawke since he spent most of his time with Spencer as a kid, but the two of them had always clashed.

Plan B

Once Camron had Travis's car hooked up, Hawke drove slowly down the road, letting the tow truck follow behind, and in just a few minutes, Travis saw his driveway up ahead. As they pulled in and parked, Spencer stepped out on the front porch. Spencer's presence wasn't exactly comforting but still better than his mama. Hawke must have called to alert him before joining Travis back in the car. The wrecker pulled in with Travis's truck and parked near the barn.

Hawke opened his door at the same time that Travis did and curtly told Travis to follow him to the porch. For God's sake, couldn't they just leave him in peace? It was hell having an older brother and cousin who were both so straight-laced and perfect. His face burned at the idea that Camron was going to witness his embarrassment. Now if his mother joined them on the porch, his humiliation would just about be complete. Please God, let her be asleep.

As if in a direct, albeit negative response to his prayer, Emma Sutherland stepped out on the porch behind Spencer, her face as dark as a storm cloud and her eyes spitting fire. Thank you, God.

****

Hawke and Travis walked up to the porch. After one contemptuous look at Travis, Spencer directed all his attention to Hawke. "Hey, Hawke."

Emma angled past him and grabbed Travis by the arm, pulling him up beside her on the porch before turning on Hawke. "Why in the hell are you harassing my son, Hawke Sutherland?"

"Harassing him? Damn it, Emma, I'm trying to save his life. Look at the condition he's in!"

She pulled Travis closer to her side. "He looks fine to me. He's had the flu, that's all, so he's still a little pale. He's always been delicate."

"Mama!" Spencer and Travis said together and then glared at each other. Spencer blew out a long breath. "Don't tell lies for him, Mama. Can't you see what kind of shape he's in?" She made a snorting noise and pulled Travis's head down on her shoulder. She was over six feet tall, and as strong as a woman half her age, so Travis probably couldn't have easily gotten away if he'd tried.

"Thanks for bringing him home, Hawke," Spencer said apologetically.

"No, problem," Hawke said, his lips tight with anger. "I could have taken him to jail for DUI, but since we were this close to the house, I decided to just bring him on home. Another DUI and he'll lose his license. Not that he wouldn't deserve it. You need to chew his ass out, Emma, not baby him. He reeks of alcohol and marijuana."

Travis pulled his head off his mother's chest and tried manfully to get away, but she clung to him like a monkey to a cupcake. "You two know that I'm standing here, right?" Travis cried, still trying to fight her off. "I can hear you."

Hawke laughed shortly and Spencer turned to Travis. "Just get your ass in the house, and thank God Hawke didn't take you to jail."

"Yeah, well, he still didn't have to tow my car. I told him he could call you!"

Emma's head snapped up, and she fixed a withering gaze on Hawke. "And how damn much is *that* going to cost? You might be made of money, Hawke Sutherland, but we have to work for a living!"

Hawke rolled his eyes and blew out a long-suffering breath.

"You know my boy is between jobs right now!" Emma cried.

"To be between jobs, you actually have to have had one at some point, Mama," Spencer said softly, and Travis struggled again to get away from Emma, probably to tell Spencer what he thought of him too.

"Fuck you, Spencer," he said in a voice muffled against Emma's shoulder. "And the horse you rode in on!"

Hawke and Spencer looked at each other and Spencer shook his head. "You know, I never understood that expression. Why the hell would he want to fuck me *or* my horse?"

"Oh go to hell, Spencer!" Travis finally wrest himself out of his mother's embrace and stomped in the house, slamming the door behind him. His mother gave Hawke one more evil glare before she followed him inside.

"Whew, I know that we're not that much older than him, but he seems like such a spoiled brat to me," Spencer said.

Hawke laughed. "Maybe we were, too, at that age, Spencer. We just choose not to remember it. Anyway, I've got to go. My shift is over and I want to get on home. Jace went to Huntsville today to check on taking some classes, and I want to see how that went."

"Yeah, right. Still in the honeymoon phase, huh, Hawke?" he taunted.

Hawke smiled and said, "Jealous you don't have anybody waiting on you at home?"

"Hell, no. You know that I don't want to be tied down to one person. I like my freedom too much."

"Mm-hm. Just you wait, bud. If the mating call hits you, there won't be a damn thing you can do about it. It's powerful stuff." Spencer shivered and Hawke laughed, throwing up his hand in a wave as he walked back to his vehicle. "Good luck with your boy in there. Better go in and tell him a little bedtime story and tuck him in tight. Tomorrow's the dark moon, and the way he's been acting, things are liable to get rough."

Spencer walked back into the house and straight toward Travis's room. His brother was already lying across the bed, the pillow over his head as their mama fussed at him to take off his clothes and get under the covers. She never stopped talking long enough to get a full breath. Despite the way she'd defended him to Hawke, she was chewing him out now, and in no uncertain terms. Spencer noticed the door to his parents' bedroom was firmly shut. His dad knew when to take cover. After all, he'd had a lot of experience over the years.

Plan B

Spencer went into the kitchen to get something to eat, thinking about his little brother. He looked young and innocent, with his soft hair and his big moss-colored eyes, but what a joke that was. He was way too good-looking for his own good and always had been. If he'd been a girl, you would have called him beautiful, and Spencer wasn't sure the word still didn't apply.

He was tall and lean, almost deceptively so, because Spencer knew how strong he was. He had a shock of sandy colored hair shot through with platinum blond highlights. It was usually too long and continually falling across his eyes. Spencer had seen more than one person reach over to brush it back out of his face and watched his brother flirt outrageously with them when they did, whether they were male or female. Though with males—especially good looking males—he really laid it on thick. To top it all off, he was way too used to getting his own way. He should have been disciplined more as a child, but Spencer was afraid that it was too late now.

When Travis was a baby, he'd had rheumatic fever, and afterward the doctors noticed a heart murmur. It was only a mild one—an "innocent" heart murmur, they'd called it, and he'd since outgrown it, but their mother had acted as if the kid were an invalid ever since. Despite the doctor's assurances that an innocent murmur was harmless, she made it her life's work to see that her child wanted for nothing. Every little whimper that came out of his mouth elicited a response, and she sat and rocked him for hours on end in the hospital, as if he were at death's door. When their dad remonstrated with her, she'd turned on him fiercely. "He has a heart condition," she'd pronounce in stentorian tones, effectively bringing the argument to a close.

Not that she'd neglected Spencer—he got his own share of her smothering love, but poor Travis bore the brunt of it.

Actually, it wasn't all his mom's fault. Spencer figured that the whole family was to blame for how Travis had turned out. After having Spencer, his Mom had had several miscarriages, and his parents believed that Spencer would be their only child. Eventually, Travis was born when his brother was ten years old and they'd all doted on him, including Spencer.

Through the years, none of his family had been able to discipline him or deny him anything he wanted. Spencer included himself in the blame for how Travis had turned out and hoped that it wasn't too late. He was going to have to talk to his parents about what they should do. His father would be easy, but Lord, he dreaded talking to his mother.

Plan B

He hoped he'd have a chance to talk to his parents before Travis could worm his way into their mother's good graces again. For such a strong woman, she was an absolute marshmallow around his brother and could be manipulated by him shamelessly. He smiled, thinking that he had done his own share of manipulating her himself. One thing was certain, she loved her boys—to a fault.

Spencer sat down at the table and waited for his mother to come back out of Travis's room. She'd called him to come over earlier, when Travis hadn't returned home at the time she thought he should, and now that Travis was here and safe, there really wasn't any reason to stay. Of course, Hawke was right, he didn't have anything or anyone waiting on him at home so he might as well spend the night now and make sure that Travis didn't get back up and leave again. It would be just like him.

Chapter Two

Travis woke up feeling like hell. His head ached and he had that dry, cotton-mouth he always had after drinking too much, but he didn't feel disoriented anymore at least. There was no sound coming from his parents' room, so they must have already left for work. Thank God for small favors.

After going to the bathroom to relieve himself, he rummaged around in his dresser until he found a pair of sweat pants. He slid them on and went in search of aspirin, water and food, in approximately that order.

Walking into the kitchen, he was startled to see Spencer rummaging in the refrigerator. "Shit, you scared me, Spencer. What the hell are you still here for? Where's Mama and Dad?"

"They've already left for work, but I decided to stick around to talk to you. I wanted to make sure you didn't get up and do something else stupid. You've been on a roll of stupid behavior for a while now."

"Oh, hell, are you my keeper now?" Travis pushed past him and grabbed a bottle of juice from the refrigerator, turning it up and drinking in long gulps.

Spencer watched him broodingly. "No, but it sure seems like you need one."

"Spencer, I'm not a baby anymore. I can take care of myself and make my own decisions."

"Yeah, I can see how well you've done with that. If Hawke hadn't been the one to stop you last night, you'd probably be sitting in jail right now."

"Go to hell, Spencer." Travis gave the insult without real heat. He'd always admired Spencer, though he tried to boss him way too much. He took his juice to the table and sat down.

"Trying to keep you out of trouble *is* hell, Travis. And just what do you think you're doing going around with Holden MacKay?"

"If it's any of your business, which it's not, I like Holden. He's fun to be with and he treats me like an adult, unlike everybody else in my family." Travis burped and threw the container into the trash can.

"When you start acting like an adult, we'll treat you like one." Just then, a funny look popped onto Spencer's face. "Oh, Jesus, Travis, you and him don't like—have sex, do you?"

Startled, Travis looked at his brother with wide eyes. "You know, Spencer that really is none of your business."

"Well, I know that the urge to have sex starts coming on pretty strong after your first shift and you've had a couple of shifts now." He looked at him suspiciously. "Please God tell me, that Holden and you aren't fooling around! He's made no secret of his hatred for the Sutherlands. There's absolutely no future with him."

"No, we're not *fooling around*, as you say, not that it's any of your business. Well, maybe we are a little, but it's only some of the Sutherlands he hates. He's always been fine with me. Besides it seems to me that you've been able to handle the need for sex without any problems, and you're a lot older than I am."

Spencer glared at him. "I'm not that much older than you, and I guess that I've been lucky so far. I haven't had any desire to settle down yet, which is good because I'm not ready for it."

"At your age? When the hell are you going to be ready? Hawke's as old as you and he found somebody. Anyway, how do you know that you aren't going to get a mating call like Hawke did?"

Spencer shrugged. "Lord, Travis, I'm only twenty-eight. I'm not exactly on social security yet. Besides, they say that you'll know when it hits you, but since I've never felt it, I have no idea. Hawke says that he knew the instant that Jace walked into his office. Hell, even before. He said he was looking out the window, saw him pull up and get out of his truck, and he just knew. Hawke said you can't stand to be away from them, and there's even a scent around them sometimes, if it's a strong call."

"Yeah, well, anyway my love life is none of your business."

"All I know is, even if you're just messing around with Holden, there's going to be hell to pay. You know how Mama feels about the MacKays, and it won't matter if you *are* her little baby boy. She'll whip your ass."

Plan B

Travis sighed tiredly. "Why don't you go home, Spencer? I'm fine now, and I don't plan on going anywhere else today. As a matter of fact, I'm thinking about taking another nap before the shift tonight."

"I hope you're telling me the truth, because I do have a couple of things to do before I can actually go home and rest myself."

"Okay, then just go, will you? I'm fine."

"Okay, okay, I'm going, but you'd better behave yourself."

Travis turned to go back to his bedroom. "Whatever."

He was already back on his bed when he heard the front door closing behind his brother. He wasn't really sleepy, he just needed to think—and get away from Spencer. He hated to admit it, but his brother was right. He needed to get up off his ass and get a job and his own place. Someday real soon. Maybe one day next week.

He yawned and got up again, drifting back into the living room to fall down in a big chair in front of the TV. Maybe he'd talk to his dad tonight about working in the hardware store here in town. Or tomorrow—whatever. No rush.

His dad owned a hardware store in Huntsville, though Spencer mostly ran things. He had one here in town too, but only opened it a couple of days a week. His father had talked to Travis about opening the store in town full time and letting him run that one, so that Spencer wouldn't have to worry about it. Travis had been going to college then and hadn't wanted to spare the time, but since he'd flunked out of school a few months before, he had nothing but time on his hands these days.

While he was lying there, mulling these plans over, he thought he heard something outside. He started to get up just as someone knocked softly on the door. That's when he felt the weird tingle run all the way down his spine, making him shiver.

He had felt something like it earlier, when he was sitting in Hawke's vehicle, after the tow truck arrived. As a matter of fact, it was around the time that Camron stopped to talk to him. He was too fucked up at the time to be able to remember it clearly until just now.

He shivered again and opened the door. Camron stood on the porch, and he was looking fine. Travis looked him up and down and felt his mouth go a little dry.

"Hey, Camron, what's up?" Travis was trying to remain cool, but it was hard when he had this overpowering urge to wrap his arms around the man.

Travis noticed that Camron gave him an odd look. "Uh, Travis, I brought your keys by. I didn't realize that I'd taken them with me till just before I closed the shop." He held out the keys and Travis took them. Their hands brushed each other's and both of them jumped. Travis could have sworn he saw a spark leap up between them. Must be static electricity.

Plan B

"Thanks," Travis said, his voice suddenly unsteady. "You want to come in for a few minutes? Have something to drink?" Travis realized that he really didn't want Camron to leave. He looked up from under his eyelashes at him, instinctively flirting with the man. In the next instant, he realized what he was doing—Camron was well known for being straight. Travis would be lucky if Camron didn't beat the shit out of him. He straightened up and brushed his hair out of his eyes. He touched his tongue to his dry lips and saw Camron watch him do it and then narrow his eyes.

"No, thanks. I need to get on home, but maybe some other time. Here's my card if you need to get in touch with me about anything. It has my cell number on it."

Travis couldn't imagine any reason that he would need to get in touch with Camron, but he took the card and held onto it like a lifeline. Jesus, what was the matter with him? "Okay, thanks." He couldn't seem to get much volume in his voice. The words came out breathy and soft.

Camron gave him one more unreadable look and then turned away. Travis shut the door and walked back to his bedroom, still clutching the card. He sat down on the bed and opened the drawer of his bedside table, putting the card in there where it wouldn't get lost. Hell, why should he care if it got lost? He had gone to school with Camron, after all. In all the years that they had known each other, Travis had never felt the need to call Camron and certainly the reverse was true.

He lay back on the bed, wondering why he had been so sorry to see Camron leave. Sorry, hell, it was gut wrenching, like he was losing something really important to him—something vital that he needed to live. His heart was beating wildly and his cock had started aching as soon as he had seen the other man standing at the door. Well, a little before that, actually, like when he felt that shiver just before he opened the door.

Travis rubbed a hand over his erection and closed his eyes. All he could see in his mind was Camron, tall and muscular, with dark brown hair cut short in that high and tight style he favored and those pretty hazel eyes. Yeah, hazel, that's what you called them. Kinda green but not exactly. More gold colored. God, he was sex on a stick, but Travis had never reacted this way to him before. He couldn't figure it out.

He found himself wondering what Camron's body looked like naked now. When they had been on the team together, he had seen him several times in the shower and in the locker room, and his body was hot even back then. He used to sneak looks at him when he thought he wasn't looking. It didn't look like his body had changed much, just a little more muscular. He was maybe an inch taller than Travis and weighed a little more. He looked like a man who worked hard for a living. And there went his cock again, standing up and tenting his pants.

Plan B

He yanked them off and lay spread-eagled on the bed, giving his dick some room. Then, he reached down and began stroking it slowly, picturing Camron's face and body as he did, picturing Camron naked and hard. He let himself imagine that it was Camron's hand on his shaft, squeezing it, stroking it, teasing the slit. A wave of longing swept over him like a tide, and he came uncontrollably. When the last of the little aftershocks shuddered through him, he gradually became aware that he'd come all over himself with his bedroom door standing wide open. Thank God he was home alone. He definitely had to talk to his father about a job so he could move the hell out of this house.

****

Camron turned around and practically jumped off Travis' front porch, in his rush to get away. He turned his truck around in the driveway and squealed tires, driving faster than necessary. What the fuck was that about--giving Travis his card and telling him to call him if he needed anything? He didn't even much like the little shit, so he didn't know why he'd ever want to help him. As far as Camron was concerned, Travis was a fuck-up who had never had to take responsibility for anything. Yeah, he was a good-looking young guy. Really good-looking, almost pretty, but what the hell? Why was he thinking about that? Why was he even thinking about the boy at all?

Determinedly, he thought about Jenny and how he'd made love to her the night before. She'd wrapped those soft long legs around his waist, and he'd made sweet love to her for half the night. He needed to get some more of that just as soon as the dark moon was over for the month. Yeah, he needed to keep Jenny in mind and stop thinking about that little punk--with his soft, shiny hair and the green eyes that seemed to glow at him. And those thick black eyelashes that were like a doll's, too damn pretty to be on a man.

Camron had felt this attraction earlier when he'd come to tow Travis' car, but wasn't sure what the feeling was until he had brought the keys back to Travis. When the door opened and Travis stood there in nothing but a pair of thin sweat pants and a bad case of bedhead, Camron's mouth went dry. He looked so damned warm and sleepy and sweet. His bare feet looked cold and he wanted to make him go put on some socks or shoes or something. He stared into those damn big green eyes of his and tried not to think about how hot that body was. And those lush lips of his…

He hadn't been able to speak, at first, because he so puzzled by his own reaction to another man. He had never felt this kind of attraction to any man before, and didn't want to now. Damn it, he'd wanted to kiss Travis. Wanted it so bad it made his teeth ache. He wanted even now to go back there and knock on the door and when he opened up, pull the boy into his arms and kiss the shit out of him, make him whimper into his mouth and beg him to stop.

Plan B

But he wouldn't stop. He'd walk him backward into that house and lay him down. Take his pants off him and swallow him whole. He'd lick him and suck him until he had him crying and begging for mercy, but he wouldn't show him any. He'd suck him down until he came--until he couldn't stop coming and then he'd lick up every drop. He'd suck on him until he spread his legs and opened up for him like a ripe peach, and then he'd show him who he belonged to. Camron's cock would push into that dark, velvety heat until he buried himself up to his balls.

He hoped Travis would squirm and try to get away, but it would be useless, because he would be impaled on Camron's cock, and he'd never get away. He'd wrap his arms around him and stroke his dick until he had him talking in tongues. Hell yeah, Travis was his. His mate.

The sudden knowledge stunned him so badly he had to pull over on the side of the road and sit there until he stopped shaking. Shit, this was the mating call. *Damn it*! Nothing else could be so strong, so compelling! This kind of thing wasn't part of his plan, had never been a part of his plan! He'd been with boys occasionally before when he was younger, but he was only experimenting since most of the clan males seemed to like males as well as females. Not him though. He'd tried it and decided he was much more attracted to girls. They were soft and sweet-smelling and most of the time, they'd do whatever he asked. He wanted kids and a sweet little wife waiting on him at home with a hot meal. Maybe it was old-fashioned, but that's what he'd decided he wanted a long time ago.

Still, Camron had always been a realist, and he'd always been practical. If this truly was the mating urge, and he was pretty sure it was, then there was no getting around it. All his well-made plans were so much smoke and mirrors now. He wasn't going to get his little blond wife and his two point five kids and his safe little life.

Camron's father died when Camron was in high school and his mother had needed his help to keep the family business going, since he was the oldest child. They had struggled, but as soon as he graduated, he was able to take over full time and things were going well for them now. Yet, it had been hard on him—he could acknowledge that now. He'd gone to bed terrified almost every night for that first year, worrying about supporting his family. He couldn't stand the idea of his little brothers and sisters going hungry or not having nice clothes to wear, so he worked himself half to death to be able to provide for them.

Camron had eventually built himself a house on his family's land, close enough to his mother's house that he could watch after her and his younger siblings, but still far enough away to give himself a little privacy. It was a small place, just two bedrooms, but it was big enough for him. He had always planned to add on to it after he married and had children of his own. His life seemed so hectic and hard at times that he wanted peace and quiet when he got home. Surely that wasn't too much to ask.

Plan B

He had worked hard and had finally reached the point where he could begin working on his life plan. He had given it a lot of thought, and had figured that it would probably be best to marry a girl a lot like Jenny, a sweet, uncomplicated girl who had old fashioned values like his own. No clan women for sure. Too ornery, and though he liked a little fire, he wasn't fond of the brimstone that came with it. All he needed to do was choose a sweet, little human female and settle down.

It seemed, however, that there would be no female mates in his future—human or otherwise. No, he was going to get a wild, beautiful boy that would no doubt make his life a living hell. Another damn *clan male*—a mating that was as rare as it was always volatile, because there could only be one dominant male in the pairing.

One of them would have to be in charge, and that was just the nature of his kind. Camron knew that was going to be him, but how in the hell would he convince Travis? The boy was spoiled and lazy and young, but he was still a clan male, and as alpha as any of their kind. It would be a fight—a struggle that he would ultimately win, but a real battle nonetheless. It would be a delicate balance, trying to be the dominant male and not cause his mate to fear and resent him. He sighed and took a deep, steadying breath. He needed to see Travis one more time to be absolutely sure. This still could be some kind of mistake, unlikely, but possible.

He passed a hand over his face and pulled back out on the road. Tonight was the first night of the dark moon and he'd have to contend with the shifting for the next three days, so he needed to go home and rest for a while. Maybe after the dark moon, he could see Travis again and see if this—whatever it was—was still there. Surely there was no hurry, despite the unreasoning urge to turn his truck around and go back to claim his mate.

All the way home, and even after he arrived and tried to rest, Travis kept popping into his mind. Lying down to rest, he willed his mind to go completely blank and finally went to sleep, but he had no control over his dreams and to his embarrassment, Travis was the major star in them. There were several hot—make that pornographic— scenarios that played out in his subconscious state, making his sleep fitful, until he finally awoke feeling more tired than when he lay down.

It was getting dark outside and almost time for the shift. Since he lived out in the country, he usually just went through the shift in his yard, running into the nearby woods when it was completed. He walked outside and looked up at the night sky. The moon was dark, and the stars looked close enough to touch with his hand. That was his last purely human thought for a while because he felt it starting--his bones breaking and repositioning themselves, and the wildness taking over his mind.

****

Plan B

The night was like a living thing that wrapped its arms around him and caressed his body with soft fingers. Camron felt free of his burdens, of all the problems that weighed on his mind day in and day out, as he ran under the stars, night's breath in his nostrils. He was running toward something--he knew that instinctively, but he wasn't sure what. There was a scent in the wind, tantalizing him, beckoning to him, and he ran to catch it.

Then ahead of him he caught of glimpse of his quarry, a beautiful big cougar, its tawny coat vivid in the moonlight, stalking some small animal through the underbrush. He snarled, baring his teeth, and his quarry turned with a fierce growl and gave up its prey to confront him.

Camron circled around *his* new prey, looking for a weakness, something he could exploit for his own purposes. The other cat was doing the same, its ears laid back on its head, its lips drawn back in a feral snarl.

When Camron saw his prey shift its eyes to the side, checking for a clear exit from the little copse of trees they were in, he knew he'd found the vulnerability he'd been waiting for. He leaped forward, taking the other cat to the ground on its back, its hind feet scratching wildly at his belly as he stood over it, his teeth sunk down in the other cat's throat. He didn't bite down all the way, simply held the cat in place until finally it stopped struggling and became quiescent beneath him, whining and mewling. Camron's cat gave one more threatening growl and allowed the other one to get up, though he backed it slowly toward the edge of the clearing.

The other cat—the cat that belonged to him now—was making a purring sound deep in its throat, and couldn't meet his eyes. Slowly, it turned its back on him, and its front paws fell to the ground, presenting itself to him. Camron's cat leaped on top of it, staking its claim once and for all, its teeth clamping down on the other cat's neck as it yowled and cried out beneath him.

Afterward, he allowed the cat to get to its feet, nipping occasionally at its flanks to keep it in line and make sure it stayed close to him. They hunted together through the night and when Camron felt dawn coming on, he lay down beside the other cat protectively and waited for the sun.

****

On the morning following the third and last night of the dark of the moon, Hawke came in the back door of the house just after dawn, looking exhausted. Jace, who was already up and making coffee, turned and smiled at him. Hawke came directly to embrace him, his skin still cool and smelling like the outdoors. The by-now familiar wild smell was still on him too, and Jace buried his face in his neck, glad to have him safely back home.

Jace never slept well when Hawke wasn't there, and particularly not on the nights of the dark moon. It was so strange to him that he'd slept alone for most of his life with no problem, never even liked being close to someone else when he slept. Since he'd met Hawke, however, he couldn't seem to sleep without being all tangled up with him, and usually woke up to find one each of Hawke's big arms and legs thrown over him possessively.

Plan B

"You look really tired," Jace said, pulling away to peer up at him. "Do you want something to eat or would you rather just go to bed?"

"Food first, but just something quick," he said, pulling away to grab a pack of muffins out of the cabinet. He tore into the package, crammed a couple into his mouth and then went over to the milk jug on the sink to tip it back. He was always ravenous after the shift. In amused amazement Jace watched him down almost half the container of milk before he lowered it to the counter and wiped his mouth with the back of his hand. "Now maybe I can sleep."

Hawke gave Jace a smoldering glance. "You coming with me?"

Jace laughed. "Hell, no. You know as well as I do that you won't get any rest if I come to bed with you."

Hawke struck an unconscious pose in the doorway. He was wearing only his jeans, and he leaned a shoulder against the door frame. He looked big and lean and muscular and sexy as hell. "What are you saying? Afraid you can't keep your hands off me?"

"Mm, maybe, but I think that it might be the other way around. You know how you are."

"Oh, and how am I?" Hawke asked softly.

Jace just shook his head and laughed, picking up his coffee cup. "You need rest now more than you need me."

"Yeah? Why don't you let me be the judge of that?"

Jace just shook his head and walked toward the sofa to drink his coffee. He made it about three steps before Hawke's arms closed around him, pulling him in tight to his body, while one big hand reached down between them to cup and massage his dick and balls. Jace felt himself weakening and groaned, stepping out of the embrace.

"Damn it, Hawke, I'm just trying to take care of you."

"That's all I'm trying to get you to do…take care of me."

"That's not what I mean and you know it. You're always worn out after one of these nights and you look it, so why don't you go rest? I'll be here when you get up. I might even come in there in a while and take a nap with you. I don't sleep well when you're not here."

"Okay, I'm going, but I'd like to wake up in a few hours with you in that bed with me."

"Yeah, I know what you want to wake up to. Now, go." Jace watched Hawke walk to the bedroom before he settled down in front of the television with his coffee to watch the morning news. He tried to concentrate on what the announcer was saying, but kept picturing Hawke in those damn tight jeans. He put his cup down with a sigh, got up and walked toward the bedroom.

****

Plan B

Hawke woke up several hours later, spooned around Jace. Hawke's already burgeoning cock was pushing against the crease of Jace's round, firm ass, while his hand held Jace's cock, occasionally stroking up and down, feeling it swell in his hand.

Hawke heard a low groan as he felt Jace began to move in rhythm with his stroke.

"Mm. S'nice, baby," Jace murmured, turning blindly toward him and lifting his mouth for a kiss.

That was all the encouragement Hawke needed. He threw back the covers and turned Jace on his back, reaching for the lube on the bedside table. Jace smiled up at him and raised his legs, opening himself for Hawke.

When Hawke had slathered the lube on Jace's hole and his own cock, he pushed in one finger, gently probing upward for Jace's sweet spot. When he found it, he gave it a soft rub, and when Jace arched up into his hand, he slipped in another finger. He saw that Jace's eyes were tightly closed, but he was definitely not asleep. He was making his little noises that Hawke loved so much, and Hawke leaned down to kiss him, sliding his tongue into Jace's hot mouth.

Hawke heard another deep groan and Jace pulled back enough to whisper against Hawke's mouth, "Fuck me, now, Hawke--don't want to wait."

Hawke slid his swollen cock into Jace's hole, thrusting upward while stroking Jace's shaft in the same, slow rhythm. He made sure he moved to brush across Jace's prostate, and Jace gasped once, stiffening as his orgasm overtook him.

"Oh," he cried out softly. He was out of breath and shuddering with the aftershocks as he looked up in distress. "I-I came…" He broke off and looked up at Hawke miserably. Still lodged deep inside him, Hawke smiled and kissed Jace's lips. He gave a little push of his hips.

"That was the general idea," he whispered. He trailed kisses down the side of his throat, allowing him to catch his breath before he took up the rhythm again, pushing deeper and deeper into his velvet heat.

Soon his own orgasm swept him away and they clung to each other like survivors of a storm. They lay intertwined in each other's arms for a few minutes, their hearts thumping together wildly before Hawke rolled off Jace with a groan and got up to head to the bathroom. He came back a few minutes later with a wet washcloth to clean Jace.

He rolled Jace over and popped his ass. "Well, I'm starving now. Get up and let's get something to eat."

"Philistine," Jace muttered, as he rolled wearily out of bed. "You think only of your stomach."

"Now I believe I just proved I do think of one other thing." He waggled his eyebrows at Jace, eliciting the laugh he was looking for and pulled Jace into the kitchen, still naked, just the way he liked him. He'd long been of the opinion that clothes were highly overrated when it came to Jace.

Plan B

After making and eating a huge breakfast of toast, sausage and eggs, Hawke leaned back in his chair. "I've got to go to the office and check on things this afternoon. Everything seems to be quiet, but you never know. I'll be home early if nothing's going on."

"Okay, no problem. I need to go over some paperwork from the community college anyway. It's registration, so I'll be gone part of the afternoon."

"That works for me because Spencer wanted me to meet him for lunch. He said he wanted to talk to me about something."

"What do you think he wants to talk about?"

"I don't know, but if I had to guess, I'd say it's about that crazy-ass little brother of his."

Jace laughed. "I like Travis."

"I like Travis, too, but he's wild as a buck. I'm afraid he's drinking way too much too."

"You sound like some old man, all straight-laced and prudish, and I, for one, happen to know that you are neither of those things."

Hawke laughed. "Well, you'd be in a position to know." He got to his feet and stretched before leaning over to kiss Jace on the mouth, a long, lingering kiss that had him rethinking his idea to leave. "Oh hell," he groaned. "I've got to go. I'll try to be home by six and then we can explore how non-prudish I can be. Oh, and if you play your cards right, I'll even bring supper home from the diner."

Jace smiled. "Just tell me which one she fixes for you. One of these days Marie's going to lace yours with a little cyanide."

Hawke frowned. "Don't I know it? If I ever come up missing, be sure to give Marie's freezer a look. I might just wind up as one of her daily specials."

****

Camron woke up just after noon on the day following his last shift, with the idea that he didn't need to wait any longer to put his plan into action. The dark moon had finally come to an end and the plan couldn't be put off any longer. He'd tie up all his loose ends today and be ready to go get Travis the next morning. Once Camron made up his mind about something, he always liked to act on it as soon as he could, and he liked seeing his plans put into effect. He'd forged this one during these last three days of the dark moon, and it was time to make it happen.

The idea of mating with another male, no matter how good looking he might be, wasn't what he wanted, though it wasn't as shocking as it might be for someone who wasn't clan. Bi-sexuality was so common with clan that the thought of having sex with Travis didn't bother him. It was the damn struggle for dominance that was sure to come that made him a little nervous and apprehensive. Travis would fight him tooth and nail.

Plan B

The fact of the matter was that he was pretty sure his cat had already settled the issue. Three mornings in a row he'd awakened to find Travis tucked beneath him. Camron was lying partially on top of Travis, his knee snuggled up against his balls, a trusting, vulnerable position that no man would allow if he hadn't already submitted.

While in their cat, their human minds were switched off, and it was hard to remember anything that happened. He had vague memories of running with another cat, even fighting one, but not much beyond that. Still, he felt possessive and territorial when he thought about Travis, a big change from before the dark moon. No, Travis was his. He was sure of it. Now it only remained to convince him of the fact. He had a plan that had come to him gradually over the past three days and though it needed fleshing out, he was already committed to seeing it through.

As he drove into town he spotted Spencer's truck outside Marie's little café. Camron decided there was no time like the present to tell Travis's brother what was on his mind. He wouldn't be talked out of his decision, but it was the right thing to do to let Spencer know before he went to claim Travis. Spencer had been a year or two ahead of him in school, but they'd always gotten along okay, despite the way his mother and father felt about the MacKays. Like Camron, Spencer seemed to feel the feud was ancient history and was best left in the past.

Parking his truck beside Spencer's, Camron went inside the diner, glad to be out of the cold dreary rain that was so typical of November in these parts. The diner smelled warm and inviting and though the grease hung almost palpably in the air, it still was a homey atmosphere. The diner was run by Marie Sutherland, a rather surly clan female, who ruled the place with an iron fist. If there had been any other place in town to go, most people probably would have, just to avoid her, but the little cafe was the only game in town. It was just after twelve o'clock and the place was packed.

He spotted Spencer sitting at a table with his cousin Hawke and hesitated. Then, making up his mind, he went over to them. Hawke was practically raised up with Spencer and Travis, and the three of them were all as close as brothers. He might as well break the news to Hawke at the same time as Spencer.

"Hey, Camron," Hawke said with a smile as Camron walked over to stand by their table. "Have a seat."

They had just started their meal, so Camron sat down with them, nervous and unsure as to how to start the conversation. He was surprised to find that he was a little apprehensive, and that it was important to him that Spencer and Hawke approve of his plan.

"You're having meatloaf, Camron," Marie called out to him from across the room. "I'm about out of everything else. The way these boys eat around here, I'm lucky to have that. So take it or leave it."

"I'll take it, Miss Marie. Thank you."

Plan B

"You hear that, Hawke?" she said stridently. "You probably don't recognize it, but that's manners. You Sutherland boys could take a leaf out of his book."

Hawke rolled his eyes, but he grinned at Camron. "You just come in here to cause trouble, Camron?" he asked jokingly. "Now you got Marie on my ass."

"Sorry," Camron said with a smile. "I just came in to talk to Spencer about...about Travis."

"Oh hell," Spencer said, putting down his fork. "What's he done now? Does he owe you some money? You should have known better than to loan that boy money, Camron."

"I didn't loan him any money. No, this is about something else."

"Come on over here, honey, and get your plate," Marie interrupted. "I made some tea nice and fresh for you." Marie actually lowered one eyelid in an attempt at a wink. She held it just a tad too long, though, making her look as if she had something lodged in her eye. Hawke almost choked on the bite of chicken he was putting in his mouth, and Spencer looked back and forth from Camron to Hawke with amazement.

"She's *nice* to him," Spencer whispered hoarsely to Hawke. "She made him fresh tea."

Camron went to fetch his plate and a glass of sweet tea, gave Marie a big smile and a return of her wink and sat back down. "What?" he said, as the other two men continued to stare at him. "I'm just being polite."

Spencer shook his head. "Will you go get me another glass of tea?" He held out his drink glass hopefully. He'd already had his one free refill and if he tried for another, Marie would probably take his hand off.

"Sure," he said, smiling and went over to the pitcher to pour Spencer another glass. Marie smiled beatifically on him.

"You mama and them doing all right, Camron?"

"Yes ma'am. I'll be sure and tell her you asked about her."

"You do that, honey."

Camron came back to the table and put the glass down in front of Spencer.

"That was awesome," Spencer said reverently. "Can you eat lunch with us again tomorrow?"

Camron grinned and said, "Actually, I'm going out of town tomorrow and that's what I wanted to talk to you about."

"Oh yeah?" Spencer said, his face puzzled. He picked up a forkful of mashed potatoes.

"Yeah. Look, there's no easy way to tell you this, so I'm just going to come out and say it. Travis is my mate."

"Travis who?" Spencer looked over at Hawke who was much quicker on the uptake. Hawke's eyebrows had risen almost comically.

"Your brother, dumbass," Hawke said quietly.

"*My* brother? *Travis?* Your *mate?*" Now it was Spencer's turn to raise his eyebrows. He looked over at Hawke in amazement. "What's the joke? I don't get it. I'm missing something here."

Plan B

"No joke," Camron said firmly. "It was a shock to me too, believe me. He's my mate though. I woke up all three mornings of the dark moon to find him with me—actually under me on the ground. I only have vague memories of the shift, of course, but I know we were together all night. My cat has uh…claimed him."

Spencer dropped his fork again and his face went white. "Oh, my God…"

Hawke put a restraining hand on his shoulder. "Calm down, Spencer. Hear him out."

"But they're both clan males, Hawke. How in the hell is that going to work?"

"I've already told you that my cat has claimed his. You know what that means—I don't have to spell it out to you. We're mates, damn it, and he-he submitted to me. I'm sure of it."

Spencer's face went from stark white to fire engine red in the space of seconds. His fists clenched and his breath started coming faster. Again, Hawke gripped his shoulder. "Shut up, Spencer. Give yourself a minute before you say something you'll regret."

Spencer looked over at Hawke and tried to take a deep breath before turning his angry gaze back on Camron. "Are you saying what I think you are?"

"Probably. Like I said, I don't have any clear memory of anything. We were in our shifted forms. You know how that is. And I'm not here to ask your permission. I'm here to tell you he's mine."

"Yours, huh? You know he's my baby brother?"

"He's nobody's baby, though I know you and your family have treated him like one. He's been spoiled, but he's my mate, now, and I'm taking him. He belongs to me and that's all you need to know."

Spencer started to stand up. "The hell you say!"

Hawke pulled him back down. "Shut up and let me handle this."

Turning back to Camron, his expression was stern. "Just what are your uh…intentions toward Travis?"

"My intentions? I just told you he's my mate. He'll live with me now, and I'll take care of him."

Hawke's face softened a little. "Oh. I-uh-I thought you were uh…more heterosexual than bi."

Camron gave a short laugh. "So did I. Imagine my surprise! This mating thing is powerful." He gazed at Hawke. "You must know how it is."

"Yes, yes I do."

"Did Jace's relatives come to you and question your intentions?"

Hawke grinned at him. "No, by God, they didn't." He turned toward Spencer and shrugged. "Nothing you can do about it, Spencer, except be damned grateful it's Camron and not Holden MacKay."

"Holden?" Camron looked at Hawke sharply. "What's Holden got to do with this situation?"

Plan B

Spencer spoke up sullenly, still clearly not happy. "Travis has been seeing him. I don't know how far it's gone, because he wouldn't tell me."

Camron nodded. "Well, that's over with. Like I said, he belongs to me now."

"Does *he* know that? Spencer asked.

"No, or at least I don't think so. I left every morning of the dark moon before he woke up, because I needed some time to come to terms with it. That's why I'm telling you this. I'm about to go get him and explain a few hard truths to him, and I don't expect he's going to like it much."

"What exactly do you mean, Camron?" Hawke asked quietly.

"You both know as well as I do that he's wild as hell. I'm not putting up with that anymore. No more drinking, no more smoking and no more drugs. He's going to straighten up."

Spencer's eyes narrowed. "He'll fight you every step of the way. He'll probably get Mama to come get him."

"I'm not scared of your mama, but I don't want to get on her wrong side so soon either. Which is why I'm taking him out of town tomorrow. I have a cabin up in the hills above Blackwater Falls— almost ten miles up in there. It was my dad's hunting cabin, and I haven't been up since last year. That's where I'm taking him."

"What if he won't go? Hell, if you get him up there, he might not stay." Hawke shook his head. "His folks are all known to be stubborn and among our branch of the Sutherlands, that's saying something."

"Hey!" Spencer said, punching Hawke on the shoulder.

"Well, do you deny it?"

"No…I'm just sayin'…"

Camron shook his head. "Don't worry, he'll go. And I'll keep him there. But he's not leaving from up there until all the alcohol cravings are gone, and he agrees to settle down with me."

Hawke looked uncomfortable. "Why don't you have a talk with the doc before you take him? I just have a feeling that Travis is a lot worse into drinking than Spencer and his family has realized."

"Hey! What the hell does that mean?" Spencer said sharply, glaring at Hawke now too.

"It means what I've been telling you for a while now, Spencer. Travis has had a problem for months, and you've been putting your head in the sand. All I'm saying is Camron needs to see the doc. He can give him some medicine for Travis maybe. Just in case."

Camron nodded thoughtfully. "Good idea. I'll go see him right away."

"I won't have Travis hurt." Spencer said, his face darkening.

"Neither will I," Camron replied, and Spencer finally nodded.

"Suppose you *can* keep him there," Spencer said. "Then what?"

"Then he stops his drinking—we talk things over and come back home. He settles down and goes to work helping me in the business. It will be his business too, then. We'll live in my house. I have a little two bedroom cabin in the woods, and a few acres of land. It's not fancy, but it will do until the kids come."

Plan B

Spencer and Hawke looked at each other and then back at Camron. "Till the kids come?" Spencer said. "What kids would that be?"

"I'd like to adopt some kids one day. Family's important to me."

Spencer snorted. "Who the hell in their right mind is going to give my brother a kid to raise? And even if they did, we *are* in Alabama, you know. Not exactly the most gay-friendly state in the Union."

Camron shrugged. "A surrogate, maybe. I don't know, but it'll work out when the time comes. Travis is young yet, and he'll have enough to get used to at first, but he's got a good heart, and I think one of these days he'll make a good parent." A little silence settled over the table, and then Spencer spoke up.

"You sound like you might…do you love him?"

Camron stared back across the table at him. "Of course not. I barely know him at this point. But I feel…hell, I hardly know how to explain how I feel." He looked back over at Hawke. "I can't do without him, you know? It's like a piece of me is missing."

Hawke nodded thoughtfully. "Yes. I know what you mean." He turned to Spencer and slapped him on the back. "Well, I guess you can stop worrying about our boy now, Spencer. It looks to me like the cavalry has arrived and just in the nick of time."

Chapter Three

Travis scratched his belly and took another swig of his beer. It was the Saturday afternoon following the dark moon, a little too early for a beer, probably, but this was hair of the dog after the night he'd had. He hadn't rolled in until way past midnight, careful to keep to the back roads and keeping his fingers crossed that he wouldn't run into Hawke again before he reached his driveway.

His luck held, even to the point of being able to tiptoe past his parents' bedroom, his shoes in hand, without his mother hearing him. Even for clan, known for their supernaturally superior hearing, she could be downright scary sometimes, in more ways than one. As a kid, he'd rarely been able to put anything over on her, though certainly not from lack of trying. He'd had to become a master at getting around her in other ways, mostly by layering on the charm and flattery. She fell for it every time.

His parents had left him sleeping it off that morning and gone to open the hardware store, so he had the house to himself, just the way he liked it. He'd slept until almost noon, then wandered to the kitchen to eat some cold pizza and find a beer to settle his stomach. He really needed to get a shower and shave, but he was still a little too hung over and didn't feel like moving. He'd been idly flipping through some magazines about to turn on the game when the knock came on the front door.

Plan B

He groaned aloud, afraid it was Spencer coming to check on him again and see why he'd never made it into the store in town. He'd sort of promised him the day before that he'd come in today to begin learning the job, with the idea that he'd keep the store in town open, freeing Spencer to spend more time at the bigger store in Huntsville with their dad. When he'd mentioned it to Spencer though, he'd acted kind of strange. He'd listened, but seemed like his mind was on something else, and he kept giving Travis strange, almost assessing looks.

The store, called Jensen Hardware, was growing since Spencer had taken over most of the purchasing. His dad would have been content to let Spencer run the whole thing, really, never having been exactly ambitious. Travis hated to say it, but his dad was typical of the men most clan women picked out for husbands—agreeable and quiet and maybe just a little bit lazy. Spencer said once that it was probably where Travis got it from.

His mom had kept her maiden name when she married, as most clan women did, and he and his brother took the Sutherland name as well. If it bothered his father, he never let on, and mostly he seemed happy to drift through his days. From the time Travis had been a baby, he'd always known where the real power lay in their family.

The knock came again and Travis yelled down the hall. "It's open—why are you knocking?" Too annoyed to get up and trying to think of a good excuse as to why he was obviously just rolling out of the bed at past noon, he didn't notice who came in at first.

When he finally looked up to see Camron MacKay standing in the doorway, Travis's mouth fell open in surprise, and he jumped to his feet, thrusting his hands in his pockets to disguise the trembling. That scent hit him full force again, and a thrill of something like recognition raced up his spine.

"Camron!" I'm sorry, I thought you were Spencer." He raked the sports magazines off the sofa where he'd thrown them earlier and tried to uncover a spot for Camron to sit down.

Camron stood in the doorway, his well-worn jeans hugging his hips and that tight t-shirt doing nothing to hide his killer abs. It wasn't fair that a guy should look like that at this time of the morning—or afternoon, whatever. "Please, have a seat. Are you here to see my Dad? He's already left for the store."

"I'm not here to see your dad, Travis. I came to talk to you."

"Oh. Is it about the bill for the towing last week? I thought my dad had already paid that, but I'll make sure you get your money. I'll talk to him as soon as he gets home."

Camron shook his head impatiently. "I don't care about that." He stepped closer to Travis and instinctively Travis backed up a step. It wasn't that he felt threatened, but there was something so…intense about the way he was looking at him. A fleeting image came to his mind. His cat being hunted into a clearing in the woods, while another, larger cougar stalked him, a feral look in its eyes.

Camron frowned when Travis stepped back and stepped toward him again, crowding him back against the wall. He leaned in and put a hand over Travis's head, standing close to him. "Are you really going to pretend that you don't know why I'm here?"

Plan B

Travis looked up at him in amazement, his jaw dropping. "I- I don't know what you mean."

"Yes, you do," Camron said softly. "I know you must remember what happened between us the past three nights. I know you feel this too."

This close his scent was almost overwhelming, a clean male scent mixed with some kind of musky smell. Maybe his shampoo? It was intoxicating, whatever it was, and Travis raised his head and made the mistake of gazing directly into Camron's eyes. The effect was so immediate and so dizzying, he put out a hand to steady himself, touching Camron's chest.

Camron hissed in a sharp breath, and then Travis was in his arms and Camron was kissing him. The startling reality of it was such a shock to his system that he felt like every nerve ending in his body was buzzing and sparking with electricity. The raw heat of that kiss made his mouth fall open in surprised welcome, and he touched his tongue to Camron's and heard himself moan softly deep in his throat.

Camron gave a surprised little grunt of his own as he pulled Travis's body tight against his. His mouth moved against Travis's. "You taste like beer and sex and trouble, boy. What the hell am I going to do with you?"

Before Travis could answer, Camron pulled him over to the couch and pushed him back onto it, dragging his sweats down almost in the same move. Travis quickly pushed at them too, aware that Camron was still murmuring to him, his voice soft and gentle as he ran his hands over Travis's body. He palmed Travis's eager cock, which had bounced out, apparently starving for Camron's touch as it twitched and jumped in Camron's hand.

It was the gentleness that undid Travis. He'd had men do this before, but it was always quick and rough. Never with this almost loving touch, and Travis knew with sudden awareness that having felt it he could never settle for anything less again. Unable to help himself, he closed his eyes and thrust his hips upward into Camron's hard, work calloused hand, pushing his cock into that warm, sure touch and whimpering just a little.

Camron gave a funny little half laugh and then bent over him, his mouth enveloping his shaft like molten lava. The earth didn't move but something sure as hell shifted deep inside him as Camron sucked him down. He worked his tongue and his lips with careful precision and what he lacked in skill, he more than made up for in tenderness. One hand massaged Travis's balls while the other grasped his shaft, holding it still for his pleasure.

Plan B

Travis was aware that he was making noises he'd never made before, but he couldn't have stopped if he'd tried. After only seconds of Camron's incredible heat, Travis felt himself exploding, his climax taking him by surprise, forcefully wrung from him, then squeezing him dry and flinging him down again so quickly that he thought this must be what a seizure feels like—helpless and violent and totally out of control.

He couldn't open his eyes for a few seconds, but as he slowly became aware of his surroundings again, he peered up through his eyelashes to see Camron gazing down at him, his face intense.

He saw Travis peeping at him and held out his hand to help him to his feet. "Where's the shower?"

Travis pointed down the hall, and Camron gestured that he should lead the way. Travis moved on shaky legs toward the bathroom, wondering in some distant part of his mind if he had fallen asleep as he lay on the sofa thumbing through his magazines, and he was snoring loudly even now. Maybe he was simply dreaming all this, and he'd awake to find it had all been his imagination, and there was no gorgeous Camron following him down the hallway.

Camron stopped just outside the door and watched him as he entered, waiting solemnly while Travis turned on the shower and adjusted the spray. He turned back to find Camron leaning against the doorway, his expression bright and watchful.

"Get in and get cleaned up," he said quietly. "I'm not going anywhere."

Travis nodded and then self-consciously, he stripped off his pants and climbed in. He didn't know why he should feel awkward after what Camron had just done to him, but he did, too aware of Camron's quiet regard. He hurried through a quick shampoo and soaped and rinsed his body all over before turning off the water and stepping out. He realized as he did that he'd forgotten his towel, but Camron tossed him one from the hook on the back of the door and he dried off as quickly as he could and reached for his pants again.

Camron got there first and held them out of his reach. "These are dirty. Go in your room and put on some clean clothes. Some jeans. Maybe a flannel shirt, because it's turning chilly outside."

"Okay," he said, a part of his mind wondering why he was letting Camron boss him around. He led the way to his bedroom, Camron still following him quietly. It would have been creepy with anyone other than Camron, but with him it felt almost helpful—even protective. Once in his room, he quickly dressed in jeans and a soft brown flannel shirt, then sat on the bed and pulled on his socks. He reached for his tennis shoes, but Camron nodded toward his hiking boots instead.

"You taking me out for a walk?" Travis asked with a cheeky grin and almost instantly regretted it. Camron didn't answer, looking serious—deadly serious from the expression on his face, and Travis applied himself to pulling on his boots and keeping his mouth shut. There was something about Camron that didn't exactly encourage idle conversation.

Plan B

Camron had always been a serious guy, even back in high school. Travis remembered suddenly that his dad had died in an accident on the job, and Travis had taken over for him in the family business. He'd heard that Camron worked every day after school and all weekend, every weekend just to help feed the family. As he recalled, Camron had a lot of younger brothers and sisters.

"We need to talk, Travis," he said softly. "Can we go back out to the living room?"

"Yeah, sure," he said, jumping to his feet. He led the way back into the living area with Camron trailing along behind him. Travis felt nervous being around him, but couldn't figure out exactly why. He wanted to sit near him and had to force himself to sit at the opposite end of the sofa. He looked up expectantly at Camron. "Okay, now what?"

"Travis," Camron said, sitting down beside him. "I want you to go away with me for a few days."

"Go away? Where? I don't understand."

"Up to my dad's old cabin on the mountain. It's very secluded and no one will bother us there. We need to get to know each other better and work things out."

Travis tilted his head to the side. He couldn't quite figure out what Camron's deal was—not that he wasn't happy to be with him, and what they'd just done was more than okay. It was spectacular, really, and he still couldn't believe Camron had come on to him like that. Still it all felt kind of out of the blue. "Work what things out? Don't get me wrong—a little trip to a secluded cabin with you sounds great, but what do you mean?"

Camron made a sound of exasperation. "Come on, Travis, you can't be that clueless. Surely you know what's going on here."

Travis felt a little heat in his cheeks, and Camron's tone pissed him off a little. "Well, we've messed around some, if that's what you mean, and...you know. Don't get me wrong—it was totally great, and…unexpected. But…"

Camron took hold of his shoulders and made Travis look him in the eye. "Think, Travis. Why would I suddenly come over here and do that? Who did you see me with just last week when I towed your car?"

"That little blonde girl from high school, Jenny Calhoun."

"That's right. Jenny—she and I have been dating."

Surprised at the sudden stab of jealousy that evoked, Travis shrugged. "Oh. Okay…I figured that. It's okay--I won't say anything to her about all this."

"Doesn't it occur to you that it's pretty strange for me to come over here to see you and--do what we did?"

"Yeah, I guess."

Camron blew out a breath. "Damn it Travis, you have to know what I'm getting at. I know you remember—you feel it too."

Travis shook his head. "Remember what? I mean a lot of clan guys like girls and men too. It's cool."

Camron tightened his grip on Travis's shoulders. "Think, damn it. Think back to what happened last night during the shift. And both nights before that. We're mated, Travis. My cat claimed yours, and yours submitted to mine. Don't pretend you don't know that."

Plan B

"No, that's crazy...I-I wouldn't! Two clan males? No..." Doggedly Travis shook his head, but images of his cat fighting another big cougar kept flooding into his brain. He saw one of them—God, it was his cougar—on its back, fighting a larger, more aggressive cat. Then another image of his cougar on its belly, presenting its ass to the other cat. "No!" Travis roared, trying to push the image from his mind as he jumped to his feet. "No fucking way! We fought or something. That's all!"

He started out the door, not really thinking where he was going, but just wanting to get away from the images filling his mind. Camron caught his arm by the front door and slammed him back into the wall. "Where the hell are you going? You can't run from this!"

"The hell I can't!" Travis shoved Camron hard with both hands on his chest and took off out the door, jumped off the porch and then ran across the yard. He only made it a few steps before Camron tackled him from behind and brought him down hard, knocking the breath out of him.

Badly winded, Travis rolled to get away, but Camron was on top of him, pinning him to the ground. He sat on his chest and held his hands over his head. Furiously, Travis stared up into his face.

"I can see we're going to have to do this the hard way!" Camron yelled down at him. "It was too much to expect that you might sit down and discuss this like an adult!"

"Get the fuck off me!" Travis gritted out between his teeth, so furious at being held down he could feel the blood pounding in his ears.

"Stop being such a drama queen, for God's sake! I'll let you up if you can calm down."

Travis tried again to heave Camron off him, but the months of drinking and late night debauchery had taken its toll on his body. The simple fact was that he wasn't as strong as he used to be—wasn't nearly as strong as Camron. It was humiliating and made him see red. Even though they were more or less evenly matched in size, and Travis was a couple of years younger, Camron was much more powerful. Travis acknowledged the fact in his head, but his pride made him turn his face away and refuse to speak. His chest rose and fell rapidly, and he still couldn't get his breath.

"I said, are you going to calm down?" Camron stared down at him and shook his head. "Okay, so now you're not speaking to me. Very mature, Travis."

Camron got to his feet and pulled Travis with him by both wrists. Try as he might, Travis couldn't shake him off and felt himself being dragged to Camron's truck. Camron opened the door, shifted his hands to his waist and picked him up bodily, shoving him inside. As soon as he released his wrists, Travis struck him on the side of the head and kicked out with his boots, but that backfired as Camron suddenly grabbed his feet and yanked so that he fell on his back. Camron put a big hand on his chest to hold him down and jerked off both boots and socks, throwing them in the back of the truck.

Plan B

With quiet determination, he managed to recapture Travis's flailing hands and wrap duct tape around his wrists and ankles, all while Travis was trying his best to head butt him. He then wrapped another couple of pieces around his waist, and taped his arms to his body. By this time Travis was cussing him and screaming at him so loudly, he pulled off another piece and slapped it across his mouth. All Travis could do was sit there and seethe, his flashing eyes trying to promise what he'd do to Camron when he got loose.

Camron looked down at him when he finished and shook his head. "I didn't want to have to do this, but you're so damn stubborn. Now we're going to that cabin I told you about. I'm not going to harm you, except if you keep this shit up I might have to whip your ass. We *are* going to talk, boy. I told your brother where I was taking you, so don't worry about your folks." He brushed Travis's hair out of his eyes and gazed down at him solemnly. "You're not scared of me, are you?"

Travis made a sound that he hoped conveyed how unafraid he was of Camron or anybody else and glared up at him furiously. Camron smiled and shook his head. "Lord, what have I got myself into?"

****

Camron glanced over at the boy next to him in the front seat and sighed. Whenever he let him go, there was going to be one heck of a fight. Travis never took his gaze off Camron, and those flashing eyes promised bloody retribution. Maybe it would be a good idea to let him get it out of his system—one good, knock-down drag-out fight and then maybe they could shake hands and end up friends.

He glanced back over at those glittering green eyes, the soft blond hair, shot through with those silvery highlights, and wondered who the hell he was kidding. The two of them would never be friends. What lay between them was too full of passion, too raw for anything as pale and weak as friendship. This was his mate, and with every passing moment of his company, he wondered how he'd ever managed to be mostly indifferent towards him for so many years until Travis came of age.

He was so damn beautiful. Even for a girl, his eyes would have been something, but on a man those long, thick eyelashes were almost a sin. There was nothing feminine about him though. His jaw was square and manly, and though he had an unconscious grace, there was nothing prissy or womanly in the way he moved. No, it was probably those full lips that did it. They had a pretty little bow right on his upper lip that put him over the top from being merely handsome to downright gorgeous. And didn't he just know it?

Plan B

Camron grinned at him, even though he knew it would make him even more furious. "You can give me dirty looks all you want, Travis, but you're still going with me. You can't run from this thing, you know. You're mine. Our cougars already decided it for us a few nights ago. Our human minds have nothing to do with it. You've been claimed, boy, so you might as well accept it."

Travis made a sound like an angry snort and struggled again to get loose. His whole body was wracked with a sudden tremor. Camron knew he was aware he couldn't get out of the tape, but he was so mad about it, it had become an almost unconscious movement, a kind of shudder like a horse trying to knock flies off its back.

"When we get to where I parked the four-wheeler, I'm going to untie you. If you want to fight me, then I guess we'll fight." Travis shifted his angry gaze to the window beside him, his chest heaving up and down. Camron knew he'd been hung over pretty badly that morning—had even drunk a beer when he woke up, probably thinking it would make him feel better. He'd smelled it on his breath. All the struggling and fighting he'd done since then hadn't helped him any, so if they did fight, it wouldn't last too long.

Still, Camron had no desire to hurt him. He needed to build trust with Travis, and so far, not much he'd done was a step in that direction. He sighed. That kind of trust would come later, he hoped. It might never come at all and if it didn't, that was all right too. Regardless, they were both trapped in this thing, so they might as well make the best of a bad situation. Maybe one day they could come to some sort of understanding, or they might wind up despising each other. But right now, he still had a shot at working this thing out and he was going to take it.

Chapter Four

Travis seethed while Camron pulled his truck well off onto the shoulder of the road. Travis had reached the point of fury where he wasn't even thinking coherent thoughts—he just had images of mayhem and murder flashing through his brain.

To think he'd ever been attracted to this asshole! The worst thing was the humiliation of being trussed up like a hog going to slaughter. He'd never been manhandled like this in his life before, and he'd always considered himself to be strong and able to handle any situation. Yet he'd been completely unable to stop this man from forcing him into the truck. He never should have let his guard down, but he had no idea that Camron was a fucking lunatic who was going to take him right out of his house.

His damn hangover and shock at his own carelessness had slowed his reactions. That had to be it. Maybe the worst thing of all was the illicit thrill of being controlled and trapped that kept coming over him in waves as he stared over at Camron's hard, brown hands on the steering wheel. His damn dick was straining against his zipper. His captor stared straight ahead, thank God, and seemed not to notice it. His handsome profile made it difficult for Travis to stop watching him. He *didn't* want this, no matter what his body was saying, and as soon as he could figure a way out of these bonds he'd show him exactly how much he didn't.

Camron got out of the truck without so much as a glance at Travis and went over to the big cedar tree where he'd apparently chained his four-wheeler earlier and then hidden it from the road up under the low hanging branches. Travis watched as he took off the chain and pulled it out into the rough trail that led up the mountain before heading back to the truck. Grimly, he pulled open the passenger side door and that gave Travis the chance he'd been looking for.

He swung both feet around and kicked out at him when he opened the door, but Camron dodged easily enough, pulling him down out of the front seat onto the ground below. He landed so hard it rattled his teeth. Camron put a hand on the collar of Travis's shirt and hauled him off the road and up the trail a ways before he laid him on his back and took out his hunting knife. Travis's eyes widened at the sight of the wicked sharp blade, but Camron rolled his eyes at him, as if the idea that he'd use the knife on him was ludicrous. He bent over Travis and with quick, efficient moves cut him free, saving his hands for last.

Plan B

As soon as Camron made the last cut through the tape, Travis staggered to his feet and caught the larger man under the chin with a quick uppercut. Camron fell back a few steps, shaking his head like a bull, and then bent over at the waist and plowed into Travis, taking him to the ground before Travis could dodge out of the way. Travis hit the ground hard, knocking the breath out of him for a moment as he rolled over and managed to get up to his feet. He was already trembling and his heart was thudding in his chest. Camron was on his feet now too, watching him carefully, circling him, like he was waiting for an opening.

Despite the black spots still dancing in his vision, Travis rushed in and kicked at the side of Camron's knee, realizing after he'd made his move that his boots had been pulled off him and were now lying in the back of the truck. His toes made contact with bone and all he succeeded in doing was almost breaking them. Cursing, he fell on his ass, totally off balance and looked up to see Camron laughing down at him.

"Really, boy? Is that all you got? I would have thought old Spencer would have taught you a few moves at least. I guess you're a lover, not a fighter, huh?"

With a roar, Travis got back to his feet and came at him again, only to have Camron aim a kick of his own at Travis's ankles as soon as he was upright. The kick surprised him and he windmilled his arms as he lost his balance but went down hard anyway, sitting down again on his ass in the middle of the trail.

"Damn you!" Travis shouted as he looked up and saw Camron laughing at him again, but extending a hand to help him up.

"Now that you're my mate, I guess I better teach you how to fight, or with that nasty temper of yours, you'll get yourself killed."

Travis glared up at him. "I'm not your mate, goddammit!" He grabbed Camron's hand but pulled down with all his strength to jerk Camron down beside him. So this was funny to him, huh? See how funny it was when he had Travis's hands locked around his damn throat.

As Camron fell beside him, Travis rolled over on top of him, straddling him and trying his best to throttle the smile off his damn face. Camron threw up both arms, knocking Travis's to the side and then heaved himself up and over, taking Travis with him. Almost before Travis could register the fact that he was on his back again, looking up at his enemy, Camron pushed and pulled him over onto his stomach, then settled down on top of him. He grabbed both of Travis's flailing arms and wrestled them behind him, leaning over him. He felt Camron's hot breath on his neck—the son-of-a-bitch didn't even have the decency to be breathing hard.

"Give up, kit? I don't want to hurt you," he said as he let go of one arm and twisted the other up until he lost feeling in it. He was squeezing a pressure point in Travis's wrist that sent blinding pain shooting up his arm. *Didn't want to hurt him?* Damn him, this was a game to him. The idea made Travis flush with hot anger, and he reached up over his head with his free hand and grabbed a handful of Camron's hair, yanking as hard as he could.

Travis let go his wrist and knocked his hand away. "Damn it! Stop it, Travis and settle down.

Plan B

He bent low over Travis again, trapping and holding his hands high over his head again, and this time a tongue traced the edge of his ear. Travis felt it all the way to his cock, which jerked hard at the touch and desire rippled through him. He could feel Camron's erection pressing against his crease, and he found himself pushing back into it.

"That's it, kit," he whispered softly in his ear. "Just give in to me. You know you want to."

Travis growled and tried to heave Camron off him, but it was useless. He could buck and pitch all he wanted to, but he wasn't going anywhere, and they both knew it. He was only wearing himself out. Travis whimpered in frustration and felt a soft kiss on the side of his neck. "Settle down. I'm not going to hurt you."

The words made his anger surge again, but he was so tired and his head pounded with each breath he took. All he could use was his mouth. "Fuck you!" he yelled, and Camron laughed softly.

"Looks like it's going to be the other way around, kit."

"What the hell do you keep calling me? Get off me, damn you!" A fresh surge of adrenalin coursed through Travis, and he made another attempt to lever himself up and throw the larger man off his back, before giving in to Camron's greater strength and sagging back down, breathing hard.

Camron's rigid shaft pressed in harder against his ass, and Travis almost involuntarily shifted his legs apart to allow him greater access. "That's it, just relax some and I'll let you up."

"Damn it, I don't want you to *let* me do anything! Why were you calling me that stupid name?"

"Kit?" Camron chuckled, releasing Travis' hand and bending closer to him. "It seems to fit you. You're like a cute little baby cougar--a kit, they're called. All fuss and fight with nothing but milk teeth to back it up."

"Goddamn you!" Incensed, Travis tried to slam his head backward into his captor's face, only to have a forearm come down on the back of his neck and press his face down into the dirt. He whimpered again as his nose was smashed down so hard he had to try to breathe through his mouth. He felt Camron bite the back of his neck just a little too hard to be a love bite, the sharp sting forcing a startled grunt out of him.

"I can lie here all day on this nice cushy ass, kit, but I think maybe it's not so comfortable for you, is it? Wouldn't you like to stand up and stop all this?"

Travis felt a shudder race through him as Camron punctuated his words with another nip at the back of his neck, followed by a long, slow lick. "Fuck you!" Travis managed, but Camron slapped him on the back of the head, not hard, but enough to get his attention.

"Stop all your cussing. I think we'll make that a rule for you, because you hide behind those words. You've been spoiled, boy, and I'm going to change all that. Except…" he said nibbling at the back of his neck again. "Except maybe in bed. Would you like to be spoiled in bed, baby?"

Plan B

Travis whimpered again, his face mashed down into the dirt and his lips smeared with it. He couldn't stop a little sob escaping from his throat and instantly the forearm released its pressure, and he felt himself being rolled to his back. He lay still, more tired maybe than he'd ever been before as the adrenalin slowly drained away. Camron threw one big leg over his waist to sit on him again before pulling out a handkerchief from his back pocket and wiping tenderly at Travis's face.

"Ah, kit, it doesn't have to be this way between us, you know." He wiped the handkerchief across Travis's nose and lips and brushed his own lips across them too. "Whatever this is between us is *so* strong. I know you feel it too." He swung his leg off Travis and stood up. He toed his shoes off and jerked his own pants down around his ankles. Travis closed his eyes as Camron reached down to tug Travis's jeans down off his hips and pulled them off his feet. He felt Camron settle back between his legs. He pushed Travis's legs up to his chest and bent over to hold them there with his body. Travis still couldn't look at him as the blunt head of Camron's cock teased at his entrance, but he opened his eyes in a hurry as he felt a cool splash over his hole.

"Where the hell did you get lube?" Travis raised his eyebrows and stared up at him in surprise. Camron held a little packet of the stuff in his hand.

"Always prepared. I was a boy scout, you know, unlike you, I might add. You spent your time sneaking out behind the barn smoking cigarettes, I'll bet." Travis huffed out an irritated breath, and Camron bent down to brush his lips again. Travis wiped his mouth with the back of his hand. "Stop it! Leave me alone, damn it."

Camron slapped Travis's ass with an open hand, casually, with no real strength behind it, but it hurt a little, surprising Travis almost as much.

"Ow! What are you doing? You hit me!"

"I said you cuss too much." Camron loomed over him, his hands on either side of Travis's face. "And no more lying. Your dick is hard as nails. You want this as much as I do, so just admit it."

Travis blew out another breath and turned his face away. Camron grabbed his chin and forced it back around. "Admit it!"

"Okay! Okay, I want it. Is that what you want to hear?"

"I want you to ask for this. I want it clear between us that I'm not forcing you. Tell me to stop and I will. I'll let you up and take you back home if you can tell me you don't want it."

Camron actually leaned back and folded his arms across his chest to wait him out. It would have been funny if it things hadn't been so serious between them. Here he was, lying on his back in the middle of the trail with his pants beside him, and Camron kneeling between his legs, just as naked from the waist down. Both their cocks were standing out strong and proud from their bodies. Travis sighed and closed his eyes again in embarrassment.

"I want it, okay?"

"Then ask me to fuck you."

Travis felt a slow blush travel up his body from the vicinity of his toes. Ask Camron to fuck him—could he do it? Camron probably thought he was more experienced than he was. He'd actually never been with a man like that before. Did he really want his first time to be here in the dirt in the middle of the trail? He opened his eyes and looked over his knees at Camron, his beautiful face frowning impatiently, his cock big and thick and hard and leaking pearly drops of pre-cum. Hell yeah, he did.

"How do you know how to do this anyway? I thought you just went with girls."

"Mostly yes. But I've fucked guys before a couple of times. I just didn't like it as well."

"Then you why do you want to fuck me?"

"Because you are different," Camron said quietly. "Special. More special than anybody. Now do you want me to or not? You need ask, Travis."

"Ok! Will you…damn it, will you just fuck me and shut the hell up?"

Camron stared down at him. "Despite the attitude, hell yeah, I will."

"Don't call me that name anymore, okay?"

A big finger slid inside his hot, pink hole and Travis arched his back off the ground.

"Are you sure?" He pressed deep inside Travis, massaging and stretching and then added another finger, spreading his tight hole. His muscle quivered and contracted around the fingers, and Travis groaned and thrust his hips upward to get more of that delicious feeling. Another finger slipped inside, and Travis thrashed his head and grunted at the discomfort, but he didn't want it to stop.

"Oh God, Camron. Please…"

Camron chuckled and swept a long finger over a spot deep inside him that lit him up with electricity. His insides blazed with heat, and he swore he saw stars in the middle of the afternoon. Travis tried to slam down on his fingers but with one more tap on that spot and another slow rub, Camron pulled his fingers away and left Travis's hole spasming for more. "N-no!" Travis cried out, and Camron smiled down at him.

"Shhh…" he said, stroking a hand over Travis's leaking cock. "Wait, kitten." Then in one long, smooth stroke, Camron sheathed himself to the hilt inside Travis's body. Travis gasped and made a noise he'd never heard himself make before. Camron kissed the inside of his knee. "That's right, baby, make those little sounds for me."

Plan B

Camron was thrusting at him with long, slow strokes that almost made him weep with pleasure. It hurt yeah, because there was nothing small about Camron's dick, but the burning and twitching just made it even more intense. When Camron changed angles and raked over that spot inside him with his cock, Travis let out a howl that probably alerted the whole damn neighborhood. He tried to hump back harder against him to make him do it again, but he had to be content with the long, slow strokes that were all Camron would give him.

Travis was shuddering and shaking all over and bright lights seemed to dance in front of his eyes. God it was hot, and he was sweating, but nothing he could do made Camron change his slow rhythm. "Please," he begged and Camron answered by thrusting even deeper inside him until he felt stuffed and full. His stomach clenched as Camron bent over him to thrust his tongue into his mouth and sucked on Travis's tongue, shutting him up as he slammed down into him again.

Travis heard himself give another one of those little pleading sounds that actually did sound just like a damn cat. Camron pulled his mouth away and smiled down at him. "Are you purring for me? Pretty baby."

He rotated his hips and thrust again, deeper, harder, forcing himself deep inside Travis. At the same time he reached down and stroked Travis's cock, and Travis literally thought he'd black out at the sensation. A tidal wave of excitement washed over him, spinning his senses around and drowning him in passion as his orgasm hit him hard. All he could do was clutch at Camron's shoulders, hoping he'd save him as he gasped for breath and clung to him for dear life.

Camron stiffened and a flood of hot semen filled Travis's ass. He loved it that he and Camron were immune to normal human diseases, and he could touch him so intimately with no barriers between them. His head fell back as he savored the weight on top of him. God, he'd been thoroughly claimed and fucked, and he'd *never* imagined it could feel like that. Maybe he could do this if nobody knew about it. Nobody would *have* to know details, right? This could be just between the two of them.

Camron got control of his breathing and despite all that he'd said, Travis felt abandoned when he felt the warm weight of Camron's cock slide from his hole. He was startled though when Travis leaned down between his legs and settled himself on top of him. His sensitive cock jerked hard in response and Travis opened his eyes wide. A little kiss landed on the tip of his nose, and then Camron's warm lips slid across his. Travis didn't want to, but he relaxed and gave in to the sensation of his mouth on his and sighed into it. To his horror, he heard another soft little growling sound come from his throat, and Camron laughed against his lips. "Purring for me again?"

Plan B

Travis pushed at him roughly and tried again to get up, and this time Camron let him. Camron pushed against the ground and got to his feet, pulling up his jeans as Travis struggled to stand up and reached for his own pants. By the time he got them on, ignoring the stickiness leaking out of his ass, Camron had walked past him to the back of the truck and pulled out Travis' boots. He threw them over to him.

"Put these back on and decide whether or not you're going to get on the back of that four-wheeler. I'd like to take you up to the cabin, like I said. We can talk things out up there with nobody to bother us and without your mama trying to come rescue her poor baby."

Travis tugged on his boots and snorted. "Leave my mother out of this. I'll go with you to your damn cabin but only for tonight. Stop acting like you're the boss of me." He turned and jabbed a finger at him. "And you have to stop calling me those stupid names. I'm a man and not your girlfriend! I'm not a *kitten* or your *baby* or anything else. Got it?" He lifted his chin pugnaciously and glared at Camron, who was leaning against the four-wheeler, watching him, looking long and lean and sexy in his tight jeans.

"I know you're a man, Travis. Believe me. Now get on the back of the bike. You've wasted enough daylight as it is."

"*Me?*" Travis almost choked on his rage, but Camron was already turning around and hooking a leg over the bike. He started the engine and glanced over at Travis.

"Well?"

Travis huffed out a long breath but came over to climb on behind him. As Camron revved the motor and took off up the trail, Travis couldn't resist a glance back at the road, the road that represented home and safety and not having to worry about resisting this sexy fucker. He wondered if he was making a big mistake in going up the mountain with him, no matter how damn attractive he was or how much Travis wanted to see what would happen next. A big rut in the trail had Travis bouncing on his seat and instinctively he grabbed Camron around the waist, his lean muscles hard under his fingers. Camron glanced back over his shoulder at him and grinned.

"Hang on, Travis. It's going to be a bumpy ride."

Chapter Five

By the time they pulled up in front of the tiny log cabin set deep among the pines on the side of a hill, it was late afternoon, and the shadows were deep on the hillside. A small driveway led up to the front of the cabin and Camron drove up and parked in front of the steps. There was a small porch across the front of what could only be a one-room house, and someone had put up rails made from locust wood, left rustic and untrimmed. The roof of the house was cedar shakes, not exactly cheap around this part of the south, and Travis wondered what they were doing on a rustic little cabin in the backwoods.

Travis slid off the back of the four wheeler and stretched. His head hurt, his ass was sore from the unaccustomed use, and he thought how good a nice cold beer would be right about now. Looking around, he realized that was highly unlikely. They seemed to be in the middle of nowhere, and this was no part of the woods Travis had ever visited before.

When he was still a kid, no more than ten or eleven, Spencer took him hunting once with him and Hawke. They were in their late teens by then and didn't have much time for him, but he still remembered how damn much he'd hated every single second of it. He missed his games and his TV and damn it, he'd missed his mama too. He hadn't dared say anything about being homesick so the older boys wouldn't tease him about it. Instead he'd huddled up in his sleeping bag on the hard ground and vowed to never ever let himself be talked into doing that shit again. Now here he was in the woods, expected to stay in a cabin that didn't promise to be exactly luxurious or even provide much in the way of comfort. And all because once again, he allowed somebody to talk him into things he knew wouldn't be good for him.

"Where the hell are we?" He angled a look over his shoulder at Camron who was unloading packs off the back of the four-wheeler.

"This was my dad's hunting cabin. We used to come up here to get away—to fish and hunt. It's pretty rustic, but we'll have plenty of privacy."

"You think?" Travis looked around and had a decidedly bad feeling about this. It didn't look like anywhere he would want to spend any time. On the other hand, he was determined to prove to Camron that he could take anything he wanted to dish out.

Camron dropped a couple of huge packs at his feet as he walked past him toward the cabin. "Carry these inside for me, and let's go in. I'm pretty sure that we're going to have to clean it up a bit. Nobody's been here for almost a year."

Plan B

Sullenly, Travis picked up his share of the load and followed Camron. "Have I mentioned how much I hate anything rustic?"

"C'mon Travis, at least try to enjoy this. So we don't have all the modern conveniences for a few days. It's not going to kill you."

"That remains to be seen."

Camron raised an eyebrow, giving Travis a stern look, which he ignored.

Travis walked up on the porch, dropped the bags beside the front door, and crossed his arms. He knew he was being stubborn and bad-tempered, but he didn't care. He was pissed and he felt like hell. Not only that, but he couldn't understand why he had a half-hard on just at the idea of being here alone with Camron. He glared over at him as he bent down by the front door, trying to fit the key in the old lock. It was those damn tight jeans Camron insisted on wearing. They outlined his gorgeous ass perfectly.

Camron opened the door and stood aside to let Travis go in first. Travis stepped inside and snorted. It was a nightmare as far as he was concerned. Only one room, it was probably about sixteen by sixteen and covered in dust and, worst of all, cobwebs. Travis fucking hated spiders. Hated them—and had since he was a little kid. He had almost a horror of them, though he would die before he admitted it to Camron. He'd just think Travis was chickenshit if he told him. Hell, he was already treating him like a girl--so he kept his shivering to a minimum and looked around. There was a table, a couple of old straight back chairs and…no bed.

Travis turned slowly to look at Camron, narrowing his eyes. "And just where the hell are we supposed to sleep? There's no fucking bed in here."

"Yeah, the mice kept nesting in the old mattress I had up here, so I just got rid of it. And by the way, I told you that you need to clean up that language. You'll be around my younger brothers and sisters a lot once you move in with me, and I don't want them picking that up." He went over to the table and picked up an old coffee can. "I'm starting you a cuss can. Every time you cuss, a quarter goes in. When you get up to twenty quarters, I'll take it out of your ass."

"What the hell is that supposed to mean?"

"It means we're going to fight again, I guess, since that's all you seem to understand. What the hell do you think it means?"

"Oh, nice. One minute you're saying we should sit down and talk things out like adults and the next you're talking about beating my ass? Like you could!"

Travis glared at him, shaking his head. "I'm beginning to wonder if you would know how to act like an adult."

"Fuck you, Camron." He pulled out a quarter from his jeans and pitched it in the can. "Here. I'll gladly pay for the privilege of saying that."

Plan B

Camron clenched his fists and took a step toward him, which had Travis turning away quickly and stomping toward the window, not feeling up to another fight right that minute. His head ached and his stomach hurt and all he wanted to do was stretch out on a bed somewhere—except there wasn't one. He pulled back the curtain covering the window, hoping to let in a little light. The window was so damn filthy he couldn't see out of the thing. "This place sucks. What am I supposed to do, sit up all night?"

"There's a bed. I was trying to explain if you'd give me a chance."

"Really? Because if you're talking about sleeping bags, I can promise you that my ass won't be sleeping on the floor with rats running around."

Camron turned away in disgust. "I have an inflatable bed that's pretty comfortable, and I set out traps for the mice. I don't want to get the mattress out yet, though, till we clean up in here, so quit your bitching and let's do it."

Stubbornly, Travis turned back and leaned on the window sill at the same time a huge black spider, its body the size of a half-dollar, dropped from the top of the window and landed for a second on the back of his hand. He flung his hand wide and literally screamed, stumbling over his own feet and falling back on his ass, scooting halfway across the floor in his hurry to get away from the window.

"What is it?" Camron calmly stepped past him, found the spider on the floor and stepped on it. "My Lord, it's just a spider."

"Just a spider? That was a fucking Halloween decoration!"

Camron rolled his eyes. "It's just a wood spider. There are a lot of them up here."

"In the woods, yeah, but not the house! And don't think I forgot about those rats in the bed! If you put the mattress on the floor, they'll just crawl right in! How the hell do you expect me to sleep up here?" He reached up and clutched his head which had begun to pound about the time he fell down to get away from the spider. "Oh hell, my head hurts. Don't you have any aspirin or anything?"

Camron pulled up one of the chairs and sat down, staring at him and shaking his head.

Travis groaned again. "Don't look at me like that. I'm tired and my head hurts and my ass is sore, and I *told* you I didn't want to come up here!"

"God, I never heard so much whining." He took a deep breath and stared out the still open doorway. "Well, Travis, your daddy or your brother should have gotten this shit out of you a long time ago, but I've met your mama and I can guess she wouldn't let them."

"I told you to leave my mama out of this! She's been good to me. So what?"

"I'm not saying a word against your mama. I'm sure she's a fine woman. But she didn't do you any favors babying you like she did. It's time you learned how to man up when things aren't going your way."

"Well, hell, Camron, which is it? You want me to man up or do you want me to be your damn girlfriend? Maybe I'm not the only one who needs to learn how to cope."

Camron got an angry look on his face for a moment and then nodded his head. "Okay. You're right. I can't have it both ways, can I? The truth is I don't know how to treat you, Travis. I never had feelings like this about a man before. Part of me wants to protect you and baby you and take you to bed for about a week and make love to you. The other part—and it's a big one—wants to kick your ass. It's confusing as hell, because I *know* damn good and well you're a man. I held the proof in my hand not an hour ago."

Travis felt himself blushing and wondered where the hell that had come from. The "proof" in question was taking notice too and stiffening between his legs.

"I've never been attracted to a guy before—and I don't think I ever will be again. There sure isn't any other dude I want to fuck like I do you. So I guess it comes down to this. Man or woman, I want my mate to be somebody I can be proud of. Someone who accepts responsibility and has some pride in themselves. That's the kind of person I want to build a life with. Does that make any sense?"

Still feeling sullen, his head pounding madly, Travis found it hard to concentrate, but he nodded his head. "Yeah, I guess so."

"And you wouldn't be feeling so bad right now if you weren't so hung over."

"I'm not! Okay, I am, but all this hasn't exactly helped. You knew I was hung over when you came to the house today. Couldn't you have waited for a day when I wasn't?"

"Exactly when would that be? You've been drinking a lot in the last few months from what I hear."

"How is that any of your concern, Camron? Who did you hear that from, anyway?"

Camron sighed heavily. "It's my concern because you're my concern now, whether either of us likes it or not. I run a business, Travis. People talk, and I listen. It seems to me that you have a drinking problem, and now would be a good time to take care of it before it gets any worse. Because I can tell you right now I won't be mated to a drunk."

"I'm *not* a drunk! Fuck you!"

"Is that all you know how to say, cause you're beginning to sound like a broken record." He stood up and looked down sternly at Travis. "That's going to be another quarter. And anyway, I'll be fucking you, boy. I think we've settled that."

"Damn you, Camron MacKay. What do you think that my parents and my brother are going to say about you holding me prisoner up here and deciding what's best for me?"

"Spencer knows that I was bringing you up here, and he knows that you're my mate. I talked to him about it, and he was going to explain it to your parents."

Plan B

Travis was furious. "Well, that's just fu…that's just great. I'm not a child, but everyone thinks they know what's best for me and that they can make decisions for me like I'm too young and stupid to do it for myself."

"You are pretty young, but I know you're not stupid. And you're not being held prisoner here, and you know that too. You came with me willingly once we got to the four-wheeler. I gave you a choice."

Travis gave him a sullen look. "I thought that we were coming up here to have sex, not to do chores and get me sober."

"I'm worried about you and so is your family so why don't you humor us and at least give this a try? I'm hoping that we can work this whole thing out between us, but we can't do it if all you do is stay high. I'm being serious when I tell you that I think you have a problem. Your brother and your cousin Hawke think so too."

Travis's mouth fell open. "You talk like you think that I'm an alcoholic or something."

"Yeah, I'm afraid you are, baby—I mean, Travis. Or you're well on your way. Anyway, I talked to the doctor before we left, and he gave me a mild sedative for you to take. He said you might get nervous and have the shakes, or you might even begin throwing up."

Travis dropped his gaze, still mad, but feeling a little scared, too. What if it was true? What if he was addicted to alcohol? He had been drinking every day lately, and feeling more and more like he *needed* it to feel better. He didn't like the idea at all, so he answered Camron's accusation with bravado.

"I am *not* an alcoholic, and I don't need any damn sedative, because I won't be having any withdrawal symptoms."

"Okay, Travis, I was just letting you know I had it just in case. If you decide that you need something, let me know."

"Okay, but I won't." Travis was pissed and his adrenaline was flowing so he jumped up, grabbing a rag that Camron had put on the table and started wiping the table down.

Camron smiled and took out a broom from behind the door. "Here's a broom and there's a mop back there too, if you want to clear out some of those cobwebs and wash the floor." He started for the door. "I'm going to get some water from the creek, so you can wipe that table down and clean the floors properly." He turned at the door and grinned back in at him. "Oh, and if you get attacked by another spider and need me to kill it for you, just holler."

Travis cast him a murderous glance. "Oh, very funny. If I see any more like that first one I'm out of here. That son-of-a-bitch was like an extra from *Arachnophobia*."

Camron leaned against the door frame, smiling. "When I get back from the creek, I'll chop some wood, and we'll get that old wood burning stove going. It's probably going to get chilly after dark. There's a pump around here somewhere to blow up that mattress too, and the bedding is in that cedar chest." He nodded to an old cedar chest by the window and turned to leave.

Plan B

Travis kept wiping the rag on the furniture, though the minute Camron turned to go, Travis sank down in the chair and put his head in his hands. The damn headache was getting worse by the minute. It seemed to pound along with his heartbeat, and it was making him sick to his stomach. Shit, he wanted a beer in the worst way. He put his head down on the table and decided to close his eyes for just a few minutes.

The next thing he knew, he heard Camron coming back up on the porch. He raised his head to look up at him. "That didn't take long. Is the creek close?"

"Not far," he said, setting two pails of water down on the floor. We'll walk out there to it after I chop some wood. Maybe it'll clear your head to get some fresh air. Unless, of course you want to chop the wood." Travis didn't even bother to answer.

"That's what I thought."

"Then why the hell did you ask?" Travis yelled behind him. "I hate this place and I hate you."

"We'll see."

"Yeah, right. And don't say that."

"Say what?"

Travis gave him a disgusted look. "We'll see," he said, in a sing song voice. "And damn it, I'm hungry, Camron. Is there anything to eat in this hell hole or are you planning on starving me to into submission?"

"If I thought that would work…God, you're so melodramatic. I brought some bread, and some spam. A few cans of hash and chili and some beef stew. I even brought some peanut butter and jelly for something quick. And some Kool-aid packets too. I usually keep some sugar stored up here in jars along with flour for biscuits, and lard and some coffee. We'll have plenty to eat. I thought we might do some fishing too. You do know how to fish, don't you?"

"Well, it's not that hard is it? You put a hook in the water. It's not rocket science."

Camron smirked. "There might be a bit more to it, but I'll show you. The peanut butter and jelly and bread are over in my pack since you're starving. I'm going to get some wood in so go ahead and make me a sandwich, too, while you're at it."

"Certainly, boss."

Camron snorted and walked out the door, leaving Travis to make the sandwiches. He located the bread and peanut butter and found the jelly in a different pack, along with the packets of Kool-aid. He went on a search for sugar and found it in a big mason jar in the little pantry by the sink. He mixed it up, just throwing in a handful of sugar since he had no idea how much to use. He wanted a beer so badly he could almost taste it.

Plan B

He had to admit that other than his headache and the craving for a beer that was almost painful, he liked being with Camron, and he wasn't sure why he couldn't stop the non-stop whining. Even if he could leave this miserable cabin, he wouldn't really want to, because he wanted to be anywhere that Camron was. Camron must be right about this mate thing, because he had no idea why he felt that way. They'd done nothing but fight since early that morning. If he was right about them being mates, then maybe he was right about some other things, too, but Travis had no intention of admitting that to him.

Travis had finished making the sandwiches and had put them on the table, along with a glass of Kool-aid for each of them when Camron walked in with a load of wood in his arms.

"There's more wood out there, but let's eat before we get the rest of it in. We can stack it on the porch so it'll be handy when we need it. Man, I think I've worked up an appetite."

Travis didn't respond, just sat down at the table and began eating. He was feeling worse by the minute. His head hurt and he felt edgy and a little nauseated. Maybe he would feel better after he ate, but right now he didn't even want to think about carrying wood in. Bending over to pick it up would probably make his head pop right off his shoulders.

They ate in silence for a few minutes, which was fine with Travis, and then, Camron pointed to the old cedar chest across the room. "We need to get the blankets out of that chest and take them outside to air them out. We can drape one or two across the four wheeler. The sunlight and air will get most of the musty odor out of them before tonight."

It really wouldn't be a lot of trouble, but Travis was feeling contrary. The food hadn't helped his headache or his stomach, as he'd hoped it would. He felt like crap, and he was way beyond tired of Camron's orders, but he didn't want to listen to him mouth anymore about how lazy he was. "Okay. Whatever."

"What's the matter—headache getting worse? You're grouchy as hell, and you don't look so good."

"How observant. I feel like I was hit by a truck, damn it--my head's killing me. And I'm tired of you giving me orders and telling me what's wrong with me. If I'm such a piece of shit, just take me home and we'll forget all about this mate business, which would probably be better for both of us anyway. Like you said, you're not attracted to a man."

Camron stared at him for a long moment, studying him. "Travis, do you want one of these sedatives that the doctor gave me for you?"

"No. I don't need it. Now, just go chop the wood, or whatever, and I'll get those damn quilts or blankets or whatever they are out and bring them outside to air out."

Camron stood there for a minute, looking concerned. "Are you sure?"

Plan B

"Yes, I'm sure. Go on." He refused to admit to Camron (or himself) that he might be right about the drinking and that he just might have a serious problem that was getting worse by the minute.

****

Camron was worried about Travis. He didn't look good and was getting worse and worse as the day went on. He watched him bring the blankets out and drape them over the four-wheeler, but he was moving slowly and his skin was a sickly white. Camron hoped his drinking problem wasn't more advanced than he'd thought. If so, they would need to get back down the mountain so the doctor could check him for withdrawal symptoms. If the stubborn little shit kept refusing the sedative, Camron would just have to find a way to force it down him for his own good.

Camron finished chopping the wood that they'd need and gathered up an armload to take it into the cabin. He put some of it in the old stove, getting it ready for them to light if it started to get cold in there, which it probably would after dark.

"Do you want to walk down to the creek, Travis?"

"No, not right now. Maybe I could take a nap." His attitude seemed to be different in just the short time since he'd talked to him last. Sitting at the table, he looked half-asleep. He was subdued and couldn't seem to get his eyes open all the way. Concerned, Camron went over to him and massaged the back of his neck. Travis arched up into his touch like the little kitten he'd called him earlier, and Camron couldn't stop himself from dropping a kiss on the top of his head.

"Let me inflate the bed." He found the pump at the bottom of the cedar chest and made quick work of preparing the bed. Once Camron finished and arranged it in a corner of the room, he went out to get the blankets for Travis to lie on. When he'd fixed the bed he called over to Travis.

"It's ready. Go ahead and lie down. Maybe you'll feel better if you take a nap."

"Okay," he said and came over to lie on top of it, pulling the blanket over him with a little shiver. Camron stood looking down at him for a minute before going back out to finish stacking his wood. He was sweaty when he got done and decided to walk to the creek to wash off a bit. All of that took only about a half hour or so, but he felt refreshed and ready to face Travis again as he walked back to the cabin.

Travis was asleep, though restless and mumbling. He seemed to be having a nightmare and was thrashing his arms around. He suddenly sat straight up and opened his eyes. Camron could see that he was disoriented.

"How do you feel, Travis?"

"Bad." He looked up at Camron with his eyes dark and smudged looking. "I-I think I'm going to need one of those pills, after all, Camron."

Plan B

Thank God. "Okay, let me get you one and some water." Camron found the pills and knelt beside Travis, who raised himself up on one elbow and opened his mouth, waiting trustingly. Camron shook his head and put the pill on his tongue. Travis swallowed it and some water before lying back down. He looked so miserable though, that Camron couldn't resist petting the back of his head for a few minutes.

Travis slept the rest of the evening, while Camron straightened the cabin and mopped the floor. He turned in pretty early himself, after laying in a good supply of wood for morning. The mattress was small, not much larger than a double bed, and both Travis and Camron were large men, so when Camron pulled back the covers, he saw that Travis was sprawled over most of the mattress. He took a deep breath and crawled in beside him, feeling odd at being so up close and personal with another male. The only way to do the thing was to spoon him, so he turned Travis on his side and pushed up close.

Travis mumbled and moaned in his sleep, so Camron murmured to him as he cradled him in his arms. "Hush now, Travis. Go to sleep—everything's all right." Travis finally quieted and Camron sent up a silent prayer of thanks for the sedative. He couldn't take much more of Travis's whining and bitching. He lay as still as he could until he thought Travis had gone back to sleep and then he eased over on his back, looking up at the ceiling, dimly outlined by the moonlight streaming through the windows. What the hell had he gotten himself into?

Travis might not have been feeling well, but still he was foul-tempered and had complained about everything, as nearly as Camron could tell. Maybe this really was doomed and had no chance of working. Camron wasn't a quitter and his parents had taught him to take whatever gifts were offered him. But this thing had disaster written all over it. Maybe he should take Travis home in the morning and cut his losses. He could probably talk Jenny into taking him back—not that she'd been all that broken up about it anyway. A pretty girl like Jenny had a lot of other options, after all. Then he could take the whiny ass Travis back home and wash his hands of him.

Just then Travis turned restlessly in his sleep and threw a leg over Camron's. An arm soon followed, wrapping tightly around his waist, and then his head followed that as Travis snuggled his face into Camron's neck. His warm breath fanned against Camron's throat as he pressed his nose in deeper and sighed. A wash of tenderness flowed over Camron, and he blew out a long breath. Who the hell was he kidding? He was hooked on this damn boy and one way or another he had to see this thing through. Stretching out his arm under Travis's head, he gathered the man closer to him and closed his eyes with a sigh.

Plan B

The next morning dawned crisp and cold. It was November, and the weather was already changing fast. The side of Camron's body where Travis was spread out on top of him was warm, but the other side, where he was half hanging off the side of the mattress was like ice. Shivering, Camron pushed Travis off him and got up, pulling the blanket back over the still sleeping boy. Travis snorted once and rolled over away from him, his whole body shivering as the cold breeze hit him. Camron figured the sedative must still be working on him, and didn't want to disturb him. The doctor said he thought it might take a couple of days to detox him completely, and though he might feel bad for a few days, he should be over the worst of it by the end of the second day.

That might be later today, considering he hadn't had anything to drink but that one beer the day before. Probably the best thing to do would be to let him sleep as long as he wanted to, and then when he woke up, get him outside for some fresh air. An activity like fishing might be good—it was solitary and quiet, and he could sit in the sun by the stream and just do nothing if he wanted to.

First Camron made coffee, leaving the pot on the top of the wood stove. He ate bread smeared with blackberry jam, along with a couple of boiled eggs he'd brought from home. He made a couple extra for Travis for when he woke up too, and then went out back to the shed to dig out the old fishing equipment. He found what he needed and then went to the woods to find some bait. Checking on Travis once he'd done that, he found him still knocked out, so he took off to the stream to fish for a while. With any luck he could catch their supper that night.

At mid-afternoon, Camron went back to the house for lunch. He'd caught a few fish, at least enough to cook for dinner, and left them still cooling on a line in the stream. He opened a can of beans, and ate them standing by the front door, watching his boy as he slept. Travis groaned a few times in his sleep, but never woke up. He was restless, tossing and turning, and as he watched, Travis pushed back the covers restlessly and one of his legs thrust out from the covers. It was shapely and tanned and covered with a light coating of blond hair. It made Camron unaccountably restless and he turned away.

Just before Camron left to go back to the stream, Travis sat up, rubbing his eyes. He spotted Camron by the door. "What timezit?"

"It's afternoon. Time for you to get up and eat something. There's coffee and boiled eggs on the stove."

Travis glanced over at them and nodded. "Okay. Shit, I still feel like crap. How long is this supposed to last, Camron?"

Surprised and a little pleased that not only was Travis seeming to admit that "this" was a problem, but that he was also turning to him as a resource. He was asking him for help whether he realized it or not.

He straightened up and brought his fork back into the house, throwing the now-empty can of beans into a trash can by the door. "I'm not sure, kit. The doctor said it depended on how long you've been drinking, but from what he figured, only a couple of days, probably. He said to take as many of the sedatives as you need. They're not too strong."

Travis nodded. "Okay. Maybe after I eat something." He sat up and stretched. "Goes without saying that there's no way to take a shower, I guess."

Camron didn't bother answering, but instead of whining about it, Travis gave a sad little sigh and Camron caved right in. "I can heat some water up for you on the stove and you can take a warm sponge bath." He turned to look at Travis and the smile Travis gave him was so beautiful it melted his heart. The look in his eye, however, held a hint of calculation.

Turning away, Camron hardened his heart right back up again. *Damn it, he would not become another Travis caretaker, like all his family, including Spencer! He would not be just one more in the long line of people who made things easier for Travis. The boy could bat those long eyelashes and wrap the whole damn bunch right around his little finger and Camron would* not *join them. He didn't want to be mean to him either, but Travis had been babied far too long as it was.*

"Or you can haul your ass out of that bed and go down to the creek like I did. It's cold, sure, but it feels good after a few minutes. It'll wake you up, that's for sure."

The smile died right on Travis's face, and Camron had to steel himself against the pitiful look he gave him. It wouldn't do Travis any good to baby him further. He turned his back so he wouldn't have to see that look any longer and strode to the door. "I'll be down at the creek fishing if you decide you want to come. There are towels and washcloths in the cedar chest. Soap is by the sink."

He was out the door and halfway to the creek before he slowed down. It had been a very close thing. He almost went back and grabbed the bucket to draw water for Travis anyway—he'd had a rough night and his eyes looked shadowed and almost bruised. He forced himself to keep walking. Travis was smart and strong, and he could shake this addiction to alcohol if somebody kept a firm hand and a cool head. It was hard to do that with those soulful eyes staring up at him, and that's why he had to get out of there before he gave in.

Chapter Six

Making his way back to the creek bank, he baited his hook again and sat waiting for another bite. Maybe ten minutes later, he heard someone coming down the path. It was Travis, barefoot and wearing no shirt. He held a towel in his hand and eased his way down the rocky, leaf-strewn path. Camron shook his head and lifted one eyebrow at him.

"I couldn't find my boots," Travis said with a shrug. "And my shirt stinks too. I brought it with me to wash." He held it up to show Camron and then walked to the water's edge. "Looks pretty damn cold."

"It's a little brisk, that's for sure," Camron replied, keeping his eyes firmly turned toward his line.

He watched Travis from the corner of his eye as he bent down on the rocks and dipped his shirt in the water. He used the bar of soap to work up some lather and spread it carefully over the shirt and then rubbed it together. He dipped it back in the water and then repeated the whole process. Finally, when he seemed to be satisfied he'd done the best he could, he wrung it dry and spread it over the rocks. He looked over at Camron as if for praise for his efforts, but Camron kept gazing steadily ahead. Sighing, Travis pulled off his jeans and underwear—shot another quick glance at Travis—and then put one foot into the clear, fast-running stream.

He jerked it back quickly with a loud oath and then after another few seconds, he tried it again with the same result. This time he plopped down on a rock next to the stream and folded his arms over his chest. "This water is too damned cold for humans!"

Exasperated, Camron shook his head. "Be glad you're not human then. Get in, Travis. My Lord, my little sister bathed in this water last year and didn't make half as much noise as you. And she's six years old!"

Travis flushed a dark red and muttered something under his breath—Camron strongly suspected he was calling him and his whole family some choice names, but decided he'd rather not know for sure. He gave Travis another look with a raised eyebrow, challenging him wordlessly to man up and get it over with. Travis gritted his teeth and stepped off the rock into a portion of the stream that came up to his knees. Then seeming to steel himself, he sat down with a loud splash and a shout as the running water hit his back and cascaded over his shoulders.

Camron watched in amused fascination as Travis took the bar of soap that he'd managed to hang onto, and began soaping his armpits, his hands shaking and his teeth chattering so hard Camron thought he might chip a tooth. He even ducked his head under the water at one point, ran his soapy hands through it and dunked it again. Jumping to his feet then, splashing water everywhere, including a little on Camron, he made his way to the rocks, jerked up his towel and took off back toward the cabin without another word.

Plan B

Camron sat by the stream a minute or two before getting to his feet and following him up the trail. He picked up Travis's jeans and his shirt to take with him, figuring he'd let the shirt dry in front of the stove. The real reason he was following him, of course, was the flash he got of that delectable ass as Travis stormed back toward the cabin. Damn it, his body craved Travis's, no matter what his brain had to say about it. Maybe if he gave in and gave his body what it needed, it would stop driving him crazy like this. He doubted it, but he supposed it was worth a shot. It still bothered him that he could be so attracted to another man. Maybe he could close his eyes and imagine it was Jenny in his arms.

Going inside, he saw Travis standing on a blanket he'd put down by the stove, bent over and drying his hair. He was still shivering, and jumped in surprise as Camron took the towel away from him. "Here, let me do it," he said and pulled up one of the straight back chairs in front of the pot-bellied stove. Travis hesitated for only a moment before he sat down on the blanket between Camron's knees, turning his back toward him.

"I thought you were mad at me," Travis said softly.

"Why did you think that?" He was running his hands through Travis's silky hair, enjoying the soft slide of it through his fingers. He bent down to kiss the side of Travis's face but Travis turned into the kiss and brushed his lips against Camron's instead. He turned a little to face him.

"I've been in a bad mood, I guess. Kind of hard to live with."

"Kind of?"

Travis blushed, his cheeks turning a little pink. "Okay, I have, but I just felt so bad and I-I wanted a beer so much it sort of scared me." Lowering his eyes, he picked at a loose thread in the blanket. "I knew I was being a jerk, but I couldn't seem to stop myself." He turned his pretty green eyes up to Camron. "Do you really think I have a drinking problem?"

"No, not exactly. I think you could have one if you keep on like you have been. You need to stop now, kit, before it gets any worse. If you need help to do that, we'll get you some."

Travis shook his head, still fiddling with the string on the blanket and not meeting Camron's eyes. "I don't know. I don't think so. I drink because it's the thing to do, you know. When I go out with my friends…and we usually go to Holden's place, so it's always there."

"Yeah, well, that shit's going to stop." Camron took Travis's chin in his hand and turned his face back toward him. "Do I have a problem with Holden? Are you two…?"

"No, not really." Travis shook his head. "Honestly, I wanted to be with him, but he wasn't ever serious about me. He took me out sometimes, and I gave him a few blowjobs."

Camron's hand tightened on his chin, and he had to make himself back off and let go. It wasn't logical to blame Travis for who he'd been with before they were together—just like Camron had been with Jenny and others, Travis had a life before Camron. No matter how much it made his stomach clench to think about Travis with anybody else.

"But it's over now," Camron said, and it wasn't really a question.

"Yeah, it's over."

The heat of the stove had brought a pink glow to his skin, and when he gazed up at Camron, his blond hair drying in wisps around his face, and those emerald eyes sparkling, Camron thought he was the most beautiful thing he'd ever seen. He'd seen Jenny and other girls in similar situations and found them beautiful too, but this was totally different. There were no curves in Travis's body, and there was nothing about his lean, muscular body that was soft. He had stubble on his cheeks and the planes of his face were masculine and strong. When Camron leaned down to kiss him, he knew with certainty that this was a man he was about to make love to, and there was no way to pretend otherwise. And he didn't care.

He pulled on Travis and he came up to his knees and turned toward Camron, his hard cock pushing against the inside of his thigh. Camron looked down into his eyes and spoke to him softly. "I promised you once that I'd spoil you in bed, but I can't seem to get you in one and conscious long enough. I hope this blanket will do."

Travis smiled and sat back on the blanket, leaning back on his hands and spreading his legs. "It'll do just fine for me."

His thick cock was leaking a drop of pre-cum, and as he watched him, Travis caught it with his fingers and spread it over the head of his cock, his eyes never leaving Camron's. He looked wanton and inviting and hot as fuck. Camron got up on legs that were just a little shaky and found the lube in his pack. He stripped off his clothes in record time and turned to find Travis watching him appreciatively, his hand still lazily stroking his shaft. He spread his legs a little further apart in offering, and Camron's mouth went dry.

He knelt down beside him and pushed him back on the blanket. Slicking his fingers, he brushed them against Travis's hole, his other hand resting on his stomach. "Look up at me, sweetheart."

Travis gazed steadily up at him, his lips parting as he felt his mate's fingers start to make slow circles round his rim, not trying to enter him, just stroking him and teasing. He began to make those soft little mewling sounds Camron loved so much, and he slipped one finger inside him, feeling the muscles grabbing at it and pulling it in. He spent long moments moving it in and out, massaging gently until finally slipping in another finger. Travis threw back his head and moaned and Camron couldn't resist bending down between his legs and kissing the tip of his cock.

At the touch of his lips, Travis bucked his hips and groaned, so Camron obliged him by enveloping his sweet cock in the wet heat of his mouth. Travis gasped so loud and thrust up so hard Camron was afraid he'd come, so he gripped the base of his cock with his thumb and forefinger and held on tightly until he'd calmed down. Travis gazed up at him with pure desperation on his face and Camron laughed softly. "Slow down, baby, we have all afternoon."

Plan B

He groaned again, his eyes rolling back up in his head and Camron released his cock with a long, slow, upward pull. Bending back to his original task, he slid his fingers in deeper and crooked them to brush against his prostate. Camron allowed him only the softest touch, because he was so close, and he really wanted to make this good for Travis.

Feeling how relaxed he was, Camron added a third finger, working them inside Travis for a few more minutes. Travis rolled his hips in encouragement, soft pleas falling from his lips. Camron pulled his fingers away then and pressed the tip of his erection against Travis's hole. Holding his hand firmly on Travis's stomach, he held him still, refusing to let him wiggle his way onto his cock. He waited until Travis looked up at him again, and then he finally leaned forward, pushing into Travis slowly, but surely. He rocked his hips and sent his cock over that spot inside Travis that drove him crazy, and Travis screamed out his name.

His thrusts became deeper, harder, as he found a rhythm and Travis gripped his hips with both hands and met each thrust with his own. Travis reached blindly for his cock, but Camron brushed his hand aside and took control of it himself. One more hard thrust was all it took. Travis threw back his head and strained against Camron, clenching around his cock and making it difficult not to join him. He forced himself to ride through Travis's orgasm without coming himself and then let himself go to join him, pulling him close in his arms and burying his face in his hair.

Eventually, he managed to slip out of Travis's body and get to his feet. Using Travis's damp towel, he cleaned himself a bit and then bent to care for his mate, who murmured sleepily to him as he cleaned him off. He fell down beside him then on the blanket, with the heat of the stove lulling him to sleep. Just before he drifted off, he pulled Travis closer and wrapped a leg around him. Travis belonged to Camron, by God, and neither Holden nor any other man would ever touch him again.

****

It was at least an hour later when Travis noticed Camron stirring. He glanced away from the frying pan and down at him as the smell of hot oil and fish finally registered. Camron raised one eyelid to peer over at Travis, who was standing at the stove, not a few feet away, humming a little as he used a fork to turn the fish over in the pan.

"Travis?" Camron said, his voice still groggy with sleep. "You're cooking?"

Travis turned to grin at him. "Yep. I watched my mama enough times to know what to do. I got sort of hungry, and you were still asleep, so I got to thinking about those fish. I went down to the stream and found them on a line in the water. Didn't take long to clean them."

"You know how to clean fish?"

He rolled his eyes. "Damn, I really have given you a bad impression of me, haven't I? Of course I know how. I mean, hell, it ain't hard to chop off their heads and tails and scrape off the scaly stuff. Then like I said, I watched my mama filet and clean them and batter them up like a million times. She used to make me do my homework at the kitchen table to make sure I didn't goof off. I had a tendency back then to just doodle on my paper and not do my work."

"Imagine that."

Travis shrugged. "Yeah, well, it was boring and I'd rather play video games. Anyway, she'd sit me down at the table and make sure I did it all. You didn't have any buttermilk, or flour like she uses, but I found the cornmeal."

"That'll work. Sounds good."

"Well, it's almost ready. I made some Kool-aid too."

Travis watched Camron get up and pull on his clothes as Travis turned the fish in the pan. He'd often cooked for himself when his parents were working late, mostly just small stuff, but he'd learned from experience that as long as you kept the heat fairly low and stayed by the pan and kept turning, nothing too terrible could go wrong. He heard Camron moving around behind him putting out dishes and silverware. Camron grabbed the loaf of bread to put on the table too and by that time Travis was sliding the hot fish onto the plates.

They sat down together and had a simple meal of loaf bread and fried fish, but to Travis it tasted pretty good. This was the first time he'd cooked for Camron and he had a kind of embarrassing need to please him. He made appreciative noises at least and cleaned his plate, which Travis counted as a victory.

When they finished eating, Camron said he was going down to get a bucket of water to heat up on the stove and Travis took the leftovers way off in the woods away from the house to throw away. They didn't want to attract any nosy creatures during the night. When Camron had the water heated up, he said he'd wash dishes, since Travis had cooked, though Travis had just as much work to do rinsing the dishes, drying them and putting them away. Still, it was kind of nice not to be constantly bickering.

Afterward, Travis drifted out to the front porch and sat on the steps for a few minutes, looking up at the night sky. A few seconds later, Camron sat down beside him, leaning back on his hands and gazing up at them too.

"You know when I was a kid I thought there really was a man in the moon," Travis said.

"Really?" Camron gave him a little smile. "When was that-- last year?"

"Oh, ha ha. No, I'm serious. See his face there." Travis pointed up at the full moon and Camron, obviously humoring him, looked where he was pointing. "There's his nose and his eyes. See?"

"It's just craters and holes that make it look that way. It's called matrixing. The human brain tries to make something out of an image it can't quite make out."

"Yeah," Travis said, "but that's no fun." He was quiet for a long time and then he bumped Camron's shoulder with his own. "Hey, you know how the man in the moon gets a haircut?"

Camron rolled his eyes and huffed out a breath.

"No, come on, play along."

"I will not be a party to puns or knock-knock jokes."

"Aw Camron, how do you know they're puns?"

"I feel it in my bones."

"Oh come on. How does the man in the moon get a haircut?"

Camron sighed. "Okay, I'll bite. How?"

"Eclipse it!" Travis fell over on Camron laughing, holding onto his sides. He had always loved stupid jokes like that, and when he was a little boy, Spencer always had indulged him by telling him a new one most every day. Apparently, Camron didn't feel so indulgent.

"Well, that was dumb," he grumbled.

"Oh, come on, Camron, lighten up. Here's another one. What do you get when you take green cheese and divide its circumference by its diameter?"

When Camron just angled him a dirty look, Travis shouted out the answer, "Moon Pi!"

Camron groaned. "Okay, seriously. One more of those and I'll hurt you."

Travis got up and jumped off the porch, walking backward. "Oh yeah? Well, what do you call a clock on the moon? A *lunartick*!"

Camron lunged off the porch after him, but Travis danced out of his reach and ran toward the woods, laughing. Camron was right on his tail and caught him before he'd gone ten steps.

"Now you're going to pay," he said, pulling him into his arms and tickling his sides.

Travis convulsed in laughter but stuck his foot between Camron's ankles and kicked his feet out from under him. Camron fell but held onto Travis so that they both crashed down and landed with Camron on top of Travis.

Travis was a master at roughhousing with his brother. He decided on a trick that got Spencer every time. Going limp, he rolled his eyes up in the back of his head and gave a little cry of pain as he slumped down.

"Travis, *Travis?*" Camron said, shaking him. "Travis, talk to me. Are you okay? Did I hurt you, baby?"

Travis's eyes popped open and he laughed. "Just kidding!"

"Why, you little…" They began to wrestle on the ground, each one trying to get the other in a headlock until Travis finally managed to roll out of it and run back to the cabin. He tried to bar the door against Camron, but he pushed his way in and body slammed Travis to the wall. Grabbing Travis's hands, he pushed them over his head, holding him pinned there while he stuck his wet tongue in his ear and jammed it down inside.

"Oh God, not a wet willie!" Travis yelled, shivering in disgust. "Shit! Please, I'm sorry. I give! I give!"

"And no more puns?"

"No--No more, I promise!"

Plan B

Smiling, Camron pulled his tongue away but thrust his groin up against Travis's. "You like to tease, don't you? Maybe I should do some teasing of my own."

Travis laughed nervously and tried to pull away. "Come on, Camron, let me go," he said, his efforts to push Camron away unsuccessful. It wasn't that he didn't like Camron's arms around him, but that he liked it too much. This feeling of being overpowered and *controlled* by someone a little stronger and bigger than he was shouldn't feel so damn exciting. He hated the fact that it did.

Travis darted a glance up at Camron as he managed to jerk his hands out of Camron's grip. But then those powerful arms gathered him up, drawing him closer still to Camron's hard body, and his control seemed to slip. His hands fisted helplessly in Camron's shirt, and he could hear the steady beat of Camron's heart against his.

"No—it's not your brother or your friends you're playing with this time, kit," he whispered against his ear. "You're not getting out of this one so easy. Now relax. I'm not going to hurt you."

Another surge of irritation rushed over Travis. "I'm not afraid of you!" He struggled more, only to feel those arms tighten around him. "Stop! Let me go, damn it!"

Camron shook his head and released him, stepping back. Travis immediately changed his mind, as he suddenly couldn't bear the idea of losing Camron's arms around him. He tightened his grip on Camron's shirt and pulled him back in, burying his face in the hollow of his throat.

Camron smoothed his hands down Travis's sides and landed on his hips, pulling him toward him. "It's okay, baby," he murmured, his voice dark and velvety. "I'm not going anywhere."

With a wordless cry, Travis lifted his lips, and Camron bent down to take his mouth. He began to stroke and caress him as if he had all the time in the world at his disposal. Camron pulled Travis gently with him as he moved to the mattress and lay down with him, wrapping his body around his, petting and soothing him. Travis lay on his back and without a word, Camron soon divested him of his clothes, then knelt between his legs and enveloped him in his hot mouth. Travis came quickly in shivery jets and then Camron lay beside him, holding him and pleasuring him for a long time. When Travis could think clearly again, he turned toward Camron and stroked a finger down his arm.

"Let me take care of you," he whispered, but Camron shook his head.
"Later. I'm all right for now. I just want to hold you." So he lay in Camron's arms and drifted off to sleep as the light around them faded into darkness. He was only vaguely aware of Camron pulling the blanket over them, and then he turned over, scooted his bare ass against Camron's body and fell headlong into sleep.

*****

Plan B

The next morning he awoke to the smell of coffee. It was still fairly early from the quality of the light filtering through the window, but Camron was already up and sitting at the table, his hair still damp from what must have been an early morning dip in the stream.

He looked up when he felt Travis's regard. "Morning," he said, a smile on his lips. "Did you sleep well?"

"God, I must have." Travis sat up and dry scrubbed his face. "I didn't wake up once." He stretched and got to his feet, making his way to the front porch to take care of business. "Gotta pee like a racehorse though." He opened the door onto a day that was cloudy and much colder than it had been just the day before. This time of year was always unpredictable, especially up here. The planks on the porch were rough and cold on the soles of his feet, and he was glad of the blanket around his shoulders. He hurried back inside and sat down beside Camron at the table.

"Damn, I can't believe you went down to the creek this morning to bathe. It's colder than a witch's tit out there."

Camron smiled and shoved a plate with boiled eggs and bread toward Travis. "Eat your breakfast and warm up some. Those are the last of the eggs. I brought up a bucket of water you can heat up on the stove to wash up in afterward—considering your delicate sensibilities and all."

Travis gave him a middle finger and dug into the food. Since he started feeling better, he seemed to be hungry all the time. He noticed that Camron had heated up some water too for shaving, and his smooth skin looked so good Travis had to stop himself from reaching out and touching his face. It was bad enough he was bottoming for the man—he refused to fawn over him too.

"I was thinking it's about time we headed back. Maybe we'll get an early start in the morning. I can't afford to be away from my business much longer."

"I thought maybe your brother Will was running things for you. Doesn't he help out sometimes?"

"Yeah, and he is, but he goes to school too down in Huntsville. He doesn't have a lot of time." Camron took a sip of his coffee. "As soon as we get back, we need to move your stuff over to my house, and then you can start working with me."

Travis almost choked on the egg he was chewing. "What? Wait a minute—we're moving a little fast here, aren't we?"

Camron shrugged. "No need to wait around. You belong to me, so you might as well start acting like it. What did you think was going to happen?"

"Hell, I don't know. You haven't given me much time to think. I guess I thought we'd date a while, get to know each other better."

"For what? It's a foregone conclusion that we'll be together. Hell, we have no choice in the matter. This thing will drive us crazy otherwise."

"Well, I thought I might have more time to understand this *thing*."

Camron shrugged again, and the move was really starting to irritate Travis. "What is there to understand? We can't do anything about it anyway."

"Yes, but…"

"Hell Travis, it's just as much of a transition for me as it is for you. I suppose all my old friends will be wondering when I turned gay, after all. They've known for years that I prefer girls and now suddenly I'm moving a young guy in my house. As for the clan, they'll be wondering how the hell two clan males are managing to co-exist at all. I imagine there'll be a lot of speculation."

Travis felt the heat rush to his face. "Yeah, I know! And you can just guess what conclusion they'll come to. After all, you're older and bigger and…damn, this is going to be embarrassing!"

"It's nobody's business what we do in bed together! And if anybody is nosy enough to ask, then tell them to go to hell."

"Yeah, easy for you to say…" Travis pushed back from the table and went to retrieve his jeans from the cabin floor where they'd landed the night before. "And what's this shit about working for you? I've promised my dad I'll take over the hardware store in town."

Camron turned to face him. "Well, that was before. Now you're working for me."

"Damn it, who said? I haven't agreed to that! You can't just sweep in and take over my life like that!"

Camron stood up and shoved his hands in his pockets. His face was set and stern. "Yes, I can and I have. And what's more you like it that way. You're just fighting the inevitable."

Furious, Travis turned and shoved his feet into his boots. Grabbing a towel he headed off toward the stream. If Camron could take it, so could he. He'd show the arrogant ass! He might have little choice in this mating, but he didn't have to like it. And he didn't have to just lie down for the asshole either. He would stay unmoved and unresponsive to his touch—and if he still wanted him, he'd have to take him. He'd be an unwilling partner at best.

As he stomped down to the creek, a vision of Camron's dark curls bent over his dick came to his mind and his knees weakened so that he stumbled a little on the trail. Despite his determination not to respond to him in the future, he couldn't trust his traitorous body not to give in again. The things they'd shared since he'd first opened the door to Camron that morning felt like nothing he'd ever experienced before. He stopped by a big tree growing near the path and leaned against it, his anger draining away as quickly as it had come. Damn it, he was falling in love with Camron—and no matter what happened, he couldn't let him know it. It would only give him one more weapon to use against him.

****

Plan B

Emma Sutherland jumped up from the kitchen table and began pacing in front of her oldest son. It was still godawful early in the morning, and she woke him up and demanded his presence at five a.m. He'd finally told her the evening before, after repeated badgering, where Travis was, and who he'd left with. She'd been so angry he'd taken off, claiming important business at the store, but he should have known that wouldn't be enough to stop her.

He'd grabbed a cup of coffee when he walked in, but he had a bad feeling that he was going to need more than just caffeine to help him out.

"Spencer Sutherland, have you completely lost your mind to let my baby go off to some hunting cabin with Camron MacKay? A MacKay, for God's sake."

Spencer gave his mother an exasperated look. "Mama, Travis is not a baby. He's twenty-one years old and can make up his own mind who he wants to go off with. Besides, I think that Camron might be good for him." He didn't quite have the nerve to tell her that Camron was Travis' mate. That might just be enough to push her completely over the edge. He was a MacKay, after all, and his mama hated the Mackays.

"I don't care what *you* think. Travis has a heart condition, and he doesn't need to be out in the woods somewhere. I let you and Hawke take him out once, and he was sick for a solid week when he came home."

"Oh, Mama, he was not. He just told you that so you'd let him stay home from school."

She stopped pacing and fixed him with a deadly gaze. "Are you implying I don't know when my own child is sick?"

"Uh, no ma'am. But…"

"But nothing. Not another word on that subject, young man."

Spencer looked over at his dad, who was sitting in his chair, hardly listening to the conversation, and realized that there would be no help from him. His dad knew from long and bitter experience how Emma was once she got started. Argument was useless and would only make things worse. Spencer knew it, too, but couldn't seem to stop himself. He refused to let any of his own concern for his brother show, and truthfully, he harbored a little.

"Mama, Travis is a big boy, no, he's a man, who is perfectly healthy. He's just lazy, and you know it."

"Spencer Sutherland, you'd better watch that smart mouth and do *not* contradict me. Now, tell me where that cabin is."

Oh, Lord, this was worse than he had anticipated. Surely she didn't intend to go up there. "I don't know, Mama. Somewhere further up the mountain. It's pretty isolated, I think."

"Well, damn it all to hell, Spencer Sutherland, I could just whip your ass. Not only did you let your baby brother go off with a damned MacKay, but you don't even have a clue as to where he took him."

Spencer started feeling defensive, and more than a little worried himself. What if his mother was right? What if something bad happened to Travis? "Well, Hawke thought it would be okay."

"Hawke?" Emma stopped pacing and turned to look at Spencer, narrowing her eyes.

Spencer knew that look, and he took a step backward, beginning to fear for his own safety. He decided to throw Hawke under the bus to distract her. "Yes, Hawke. He said it would be fine. He said that Camron was a good guy, responsible and hard-working."

"And a MacKay. Anyway, do you think that I give a damn what Hawke Sutherland had to say on the subject? I'll tell you what, I could whip both your asses, and I just might do it before this is all over."

Spencer was really squirming now, under his mother's intense stare. "I'll try to find out where the cabin is, Mama, and go check on Travis."

"Never you mind. I'll take care of this myself. I think that you've done quite enough, don't you?" Emma turned on her heel and headed for the front door.

"Mama, where are you going?"

"I'm going to get my boy."

"You don't even know where to look. Why don't you let Hawke and me find out where the cabin is and go check on him, like I said a minute ago?"

She stopped and gave Spencer a look that could wither an oak tree. "You and Hawke both better back off and let me handle this, if you know what's good for you."

"Hawke is the sheriff, Mama. If there is a problem, he should be the one to take care of it."

"Yeah, he's done such a good job so far." With that parting shot, Emma went out the front door, slamming it behind her.

Spencer looked over at his father, still sitting in his easy chair, not saying a word. "Thanks for all the support, Dad."

"You know your mother, son. When she gets like that, there ain't no point in arguing with her. I've lived with her for over thirty years, and I know when to keep my mouth shut. What I don't understand is why you don't."

"I do know, Dad, but I was trying to prepare her for the rest of it. I was going to let this sink in with her and then tell her—you know—what else is going on."

"What are you talking about, son?"

"I'll tell you, Dad, but I don't think that we should tell Mama yet. The thing is, well, Travis and Camron are…mates."

"That's impossible. They're both clan males. Not only that, Camron is a MacKay. That would just be a mess."

"It's not impossible, but it is a mess. That's why I wanted to ease Mama into it, so don't tell her."

"Oh, trust me, I have no intention of telling her. You can handle that job all by yourself."

Spencer sighed. Just the thought of her reaction to this news was giving him cold chills.

"I'm going to go see Hawke and see if he'll go with me to find that damned cabin. Maybe we can warn them at least. I'll let you know if we find out anything."

Chapter Seven

Hawk was drinking his first cup of coffee, and Jace was at the kitchen table playing on his computer, when they heard a car coming up the driveway. Hawke walked over to the front window to look out. "What the hell? Looks like Spencer's car, and he's flying in here like the hounds of hell are chasing him. I wonder if something has happened."

He watched Spencer jump out of his car as soon as he stopped and bound up the front steps. Hawke opened the door just as Spencer got to it. "What the hell is going on, Spencer? Is everything okay?"

"No, everything is not okay. I told Mama about Travis going to the cabin with Camron and she lost her mind. Damn, I don't know how I'm going to tell her about the mate thing."

Jace was still sitting at the table, but looked up in surprise. "What mate thing?"

Still focused on Spencer, Hawke didn't take the time to answer Jace. Frowning, he continued to stare at his cousin. "You have to tell her, Spencer. For God's sake, they'll be living together when they get back from the cabin, I imagine. She's bound to notice a little detail like that."

"What mate thing?" Jace said again, and this time he got up and came to stand next to the two men. He pulled on Hawke's arm. "Let's try this again--what mate thing?"

When Jace walked up, Hawke had absent-mindedly put his arm around him and pulled him close. Now, he looked down at Jace as it finally registered with him that he was there. "What, baby? Did you say something?"

"Uh...*yes*. I asked you, what mate thing?"

"Oh, damn, I forgot to tell you. Camron told Spencer and me that Travis is his mate."

"Holy shit! How is that going to work? I thought that Camron was dating that Jenny girl and Travis was seeing Holden MacKay."

"Yes, but if and when the mating urge hits, there isn't much that you can do about it." He quirked an eyebrow at Jace. "You may remember how that goes."

Jace laughed. "Oh, yeah, I seem to remember something about that."

Hawke smiled. "Anyway, Camron took Travis to some hunting cabin that belongs to his family to talk to him and, you know, *bond* with him." He waggled his eyebrows and laughed.

Spencer hissed in a breath at that. "Lord, Hawke, this is my little brother you're talking about! And Mama is thoroughly pissed that I allowed this to happen."

"You didn't allow it to happen, Travis did. He's a grown man and can make his own decisions. I'm sure that if he hadn't wanted to go, Camron wouldn't have kidnapped him. Your mama's going to have to realize that Travis is not a child anymore."

"Yeah, well, that's not likely to happen anytime soon. Oh, and, by the way, she's none too happy with you right now, either."

"Me? What did I do?"

"Well. I just happened to mention that you were there when Camron told us that he wanted to take Travis to the cabin, and that you had said that Camron was a good guy, trustworthy and responsible."

"Thanks a lot. All I need is Aunt Emma being mad at me."

"Yeah, she said that she ought to whip both our asses."

"Well, she did that plenty when we were growing up, and I don't remember it as a pleasant experience. Where is she now?"

"She left, saying that she was going to get her boy, but she doesn't even know where the cabin is. I thought that maybe you and I could find out if Camron's mother knows how to get to it, and maybe we could go up there and check on things, maybe head her off."

"Okay. If we're going farther up the mountain, though, I'll need my four-wheeler."

Jace had been standing with Hawke and Spencer, listening to this conversation and chuckling at their fear of Emma Sutherland. "Can I go?" I'd like to get out for a while, and a ride up the mountain would be fun. Besides, I'd like to see Travis. I haven't seen him for a while."

Hawke looked down at Jace. "Sure. Why not? There's no real danger up there, except for Emma, of course. Anyway, she doesn't have a problem with you. It's Camron, Spencer and me that have to worry about her."

Hawke told Jace to get ready while he went to the garage and got his four-wheeler out. That done, Hawke went inside the house and came out with two deer rifles, giving one to Spencer.

"We'll take these just in case. You never know what you might run into up there, and it's better to be safe than sorry." Jace had packed them a quick lunch and brought it, along with some water bottles as he joined them. It was a raw kind of day, but Hawke saw that he'd put on his heavy jacket, so they were ready to ride. They climbed onto Hawke's SUV as Spencer kicked his starter nearby and they all headed toward the MacKay home place.

****

Emma couldn't remember the last time she'd been so mad. What the hell had Spencer been thinking, saying that it was okay for Travis to go off with Camron MacKay? Well, she'd take care of him later, him and his cousin Hawke. Thanks to them, she was on her way to Camron's mother's house to talk to a woman she'd never spoken to before—and a MacKay at that.

Emma was trying to pull herself together before she got there because she needed information from the woman and was more likely to get it if she could be nice. Her grandmother had always told her you could catch more flies with honey than with vinegar, usually after seeing Emma be rude to someone.

Plan B

She pulled up to the MacKay home and got out, looking around. It was a nice house, with a neat, well-kept yard. In the distance, she could just make out another smaller house back in the trees and wondered who lived there.

She walked up on the porch and knocked on the door, which was opened almost immediately by a middle-aged woman that Emma assumed was Camron's mother. "Mrs. MacKay?" The woman nodded. "I'm Emma Sutherland. I'm sorry to bother you, but it seems that my youngest son has gone to a cabin on the mountain with your son, Camron, and I need to know how to get there." She paused, then as an afterthought hit her. "Please."

"Is something wrong?"

"No, no. My son just forgot some medicine that he has to take every day for his heart, and I was going to take it to him."

"I'd be glad to get one of my other sons to take it up there for you on our four-wheeler."

"No, that's not necessary. I'd really rather go up there myself. I didn't know it would be necessary to have an ATV, though." She frowned, but squared her shoulders and nodded. "That's fine though. I'll call my husband to bring ours. It shouldn't take too long." She put a hand to her forehead. "I'm sure he'll be fine. It's just—you know how young boys are. He might pretend not to need it so he won't be embarrassed in front of his friends. I just hope it doesn't bring on another attack."

"My goodness. Well, you're welcome to use ours, if you feel that you have to get there quickly. Now, you just go past my son's house over there, and you'll see a trail leading off into the woods. That's the trail that will eventually lead up to the cabin. You'll come to a fork in the road about two miles down and take the right fork, up the mountain. Now as I recall there are a few more forks in that trail, but you just keep to the right. You'll come out right in front of the cabin eventually. If you'll meet me around back, I'll give you the keys. You can just leave your car in the backyard."

Emma thanked Mrs. MacKay and took off back to her car to take it around back. For a MacKay, Camron's mother was pretty nice. She wasn't clan though, so she must have married in and managed to stay mostly unaffected by them. Then too, maybe that old adage of her grandmother's about the honey and vinegar worked, after all.

****

Hawke, Jace and Spencer were quiet as they pulled their four-wheelers into the MacKay driveway until Spencer suddenly slammed his hand down on the dash and pointed. He yelled out over the roar of the motors. "Goddammit, Hawke, there's Mama's car parked in the back. She beat us here."

"Yeah, I see that. Wonder if she's still here? Y'all wait right here and I'll go see." Hawke got out of his vehicle and walked up on the porch just as the front door opened and Camron's mother pushed open the screen door.

"Lord, Sheriff, I've sure had a lot of company today."

"I see Emma Sutherland's vehicle out back. Is she still here?"

"No. She said that she had some heart medicine that her boy who's up there with Camron needed. I loaned her one of our four-wheelers to take it to him. I offered to get Will to take it, but she said no. I figured that she wanted to see for herself that he was okay. How old is that boy, anyway, and why in the world did Camron take a young kid like that up there?"

"Uh...he's not exactly a kid, Mrs. MacKay--he's twenty-one years old. It's kind of a long story--I think that he and Camron just went up there to spend some time together."

"Well, my stars. Why would his mother be so concerned about him then?"

"It's nothing for you to worry about Mrs. MacKay. I'll just go on up behind her and make sure everything's all right. So how long has she been gone?"

"About thirty or forty minutes, I reckon. I'm not sure that I gave her real good directions. I haven't been up there in a while."

Just give me the same directions you gave her, and we'll go check on things."

She told him how to get there and he went back to his ATV and climbed on. Starting the engine, he grinned over at Spencer. "She's been here all right. And now she's on her way up to save the day."

Spencer covered his eyes for a moment with one hand and groaned. Jace leaned forward from behind him, putting a hand on Hawke's shoulder. "Oh, c'mon, she's just one older lady. How bad could it get?"

Hawke laughed out loud and patted Jace's hand. "You have no idea, baby. You have no idea."

****

Emma saw what looked like a small shack way up the trail and headed for it. Surely her baby was not staying in a hovel like that. As she got closer, she saw that it was indeed a small, one-room cabin, and that it was a bit bigger than she'd thought when she first saw it, but not by much. Still, it was pretty rustic and she was certain that Travis would be glad to see her and would welcome a ride down the mountain after she'd given that man who'd taken him here a piece of her mind. Maybe a swift kick in the balls as a remembrance, while she was at it.

When she reached the cabin, she got off the four-wheeler and walked toward the front door. On the way she passed a wood pile and picked up a stout piece of wood that fit her hand just right. She didn't know what she might face inside, and she wanted to be ready. Walking up to the front door she flung it open without knocking.

Plan B

A young man who was *not* her son had his back to her and was bent over putting wood in the stove. He wasn't wearing a shirt and an ugly suspicion presented itself to her. She raked a glance around the room and saw the one mattress on the floor with the covers askew. She whirled around to face the man who had straightened and turned to face her.

"Camron MacKay! You son-of-a-bitch!" She brandished her makeshift club at him and bared her teeth.

"Mrs. Sutherland, what are you doing here? How the hell did you get up here?"

"I rode a four-wheeler up here. What do you think? And I've come to take my son home."

Emma could see confusion and anger blossoming on Camron's face as he looked from the club back to her. He folded his arms across his chest and glared back at her. "What the hell are you talking about? And you better put that thing down before you hurt yourself."

"Humph! Hurt you, more likely! Now where is my son? I know you kidnapped him and brought him up to this god-forsaken place. I swear, I'll have you arrested for this, Camron MacKay if I don't beat you to death myself first!"

"Now, you just wait a minute, Mrs. Sutherland. I did *not* kidnap Travis. He came with me of his own free will."

Emma gave him a scornful look of disbelief. "Humph! Like I'd believe the word of a kidnapper! Now where is he? Tell me, by God or I'll…" She swung the piece of wood at him and was shocked when he caught it and pulled it out of her hands like it was only a twig. He threw it across the room and then stepped out of her reach when she came at him.

"Calm down, Mrs. Sutherland. I'm not going to fight you!"

"Then tell me where my son is! Do you have him tied up somewhere?"

Camron rolled his eyes. "Don't be ridiculous. He went down to the creek, I think."

"Down to the creek? I hope he's not in that icy water. He has a heart condition, you know. I can't believe that you would just let him go off by himself like that!"

"He's not a child, ma'am, and he's perfectly fine. As a matter of fact, I'd say he's in a damn sight better shape now than he was when we first came up here."

Emma could see that Camron was angry, but she didn't care--she was way ahead of him. She watched him as he snatched a t-shirt up and pulled it over his head, noticing that his face was hard and set. He wasn't responding to her the way her sons and her husband always did and for the first time she felt a bit of grudging respect, even if he was a MacKay.

"Where is this damn creek?"

"Not far. If you'll just wait a minute, I'll go get him."

"No, you just never mind. I'll go get him myself."

Plan B

She knew that Camron was about to argue the point, but she was determined to go herself and she was about to say so when the door opened and Travis stood there with a dumbfounded look on his face.

****

Travis heard the sound of the four-wheeler from where he sat on the rocks by the creek and stood up to see who had come up the trail. As he got closer, he saw a four-wheeler parked close to the porch, and wondering who it could be, he ran up to the door and pushed it open. When he saw his mother standing there he could hardly believe his eyes. She stood on one side of the table with Camron on the other, and neither one looked very happy. As a matter of fact, Camron looked to Travis as if his head might explode at any minute. As for his mother, she had that look of righteous anger that he'd only witnessed on a few memorable and unhappy occasions. When she got like this she reminded him of an old-time runaway freight train and right now she was roaring down the track with a full head of steam.

Travis turned first toward his mother, still trying to wrap his mind around the idea that she was really here. "Mama, what the hell?"

"I've come to rescue you from this kidnapper, son."

Travis' mouth fell open and he looked over at Camron, watching him ball his hands into fists while his face got even redder--so red, in fact, that Travis was afraid Camron might be about to have a stroke. Travis took a step past his mother, dodging her arms as she reached for him and stood beside Camron with a restraining hand on his shoulder. "Please, Camron. Let me handle this."

Camron looked at him and nodded uncertainly, looking like he wanted to argue. Travis turned back to his mother and took a deep breath. First of all, he'd never been so embarrassed in his life and was furious at his mother for being here. Then too, he was more than a little concerned at what his mother's reaction would be when he told her that he had no intention of leaving until Camron did. One thing he knew for sure was that she was not going to like it and that the next few minutes were going to be very unpleasant.

"Mama, don't be silly. Camron didn't kidnap me, and surely you know that. He asked me to come up here with him and I came. It's as simple as that."

"Why, Travis? Tell me that. First, you were hanging out with that Holden MacKay and now here you are with Camron MacKay. What is it with you and these MacKays? Have they brainwashed you or something?"

He heard Camron make a snorting noise behind him. "Hell, no. Do you know how crazy that sounds? Don't you think I have enough sense to decide where I want to go and who I want to go with? I'm not stupid, Mama, and I'm not some kid."

"I know that you're not stupid, but you are my baby."

Travis groaned, summoning all the courage he could muster. He needed to make a stand right now, but he wasn't sure that he could do it. His mother was a formidable opponent, and not even his father or brother wanted to go up against her. He glanced back at Camron and then over at his mother. He had to do this. "Mama, I'm *not* leaving. Just get that idea out of your head now. I should have sent you a note or something, but I thought Spencer would tell you I was fine. I'll stay here with Camron until he's ready to go, and I'll come back with him."

He waited for the explosion and couldn't believe it when his mother just stood there with her mouth open. He had never experienced an occasion before when his mother was speechless. The three of them stood there in silence, each waiting for the other to speak, and Travis felt Camron's hand settle on his lower back. Its warmth gave him courage. He looked back at Camron, who gave him a tight little smile, and Travis stood straighter, feeling proud of himself for having the strength to stand up to his mother for a change.

Emma frowned at both Travis and Camron as she finally found her voice. "Oh, hell, no you're not! You're coming home with me, young man. Now you get out there on that four-wheeler. I'm taking you home!"

"No, Mama, you're not. I'm right where I want to be and where I belong." He took a deep breath, deciding he might as well tell her everything. "I'm not leaving Camron, Mama, because-because he's my mate, and we belong together. That's all there is to it and this is the end of the discussion."

"Y-Your mate? Another clan male? And a MacKay? Travis, have you completely lost your mind?"

Travis shook his head firmly. "No ma'am, and there's no use discussing this further. It's the mating urge, and you know as well as I do there's no fighting it even if you want to—and I don't." His could feel his face getting hotter but he kept doggedly on. "Camron has already…claimed me. There's no going back from this point. When I get back, I'll be moving in with him."

Emma staggered back a step or two and glared first at Camron and then at Travis. She sank down onto a chair at the table and nodded her head. There was a long silence and then she glared back up at Camron. "You'd better be good to him, you hear me?"

Camron nodded solemnly. "Yes ma'am. I will."

She turned back to Travis. "And you! You got to stop all that running around now and settle down. Don't shame the family in front of those MacKays."

"I will…I mean, I won't. I mean, oh hell…"

"I don't know how I'm going to tell your father—and Spencer! He'll be shocked."

"Spencer already knows. Camron told him."

Emma had grown pale as she sat at the table, but the color flew back into her cheeks now. "Spencer? Your *brother*, Spencer? He knew about this mate thing?"

"Yeah, Mama, he knew. Camron told him before we came up here."

Plan B

She made a sputtering sound that Travis knew didn't bode well for his brother. "You wait until I get my hands on that boy. Both of my boys have turned on me, keeping secrets from their own mother. After all I've done for you both!"

Travis saw tears in her eyes, signaling her move to yet another tactic. He steeled himself against this ploy, knowing that's what it was. He had seen Emma use tears many times when nothing else worked. He needed to get her out of there, and fast, before she got to him. He pointed toward the door. "You need to go on home, now, Mama. You've found out that I'm fine, and that's all you needed to know. Go on before it gets late. Can you find your way back down, or do you need help to make sure you get on the right trail?"

Wiping her eyes, she glanced up, a calculating gleam in her eye. "You know, I'm not sure. I might need you to take me back down. I don't see as well as I used to. I'm getting older, you know."

Travis sighed. He knew what she was up to and wasn't going to fall for it. "Camron would be happy to show you the way back down, won't you, Camron?"

Camron smiled. "Of course."

Emma glared at them. "Never mind! I found my way up here, and I can find my way back down. Don't worry about *me*— I'm just the woman who brought you into the world." She sniffed and walked to the door, turning to look back at Travis. "I hope you're happy. You've broken my heart."

Travis rolled his eyes. "Oh Mama, it's not like you're never going to see me again. We'll be home in a couple of days. I love you. Now be careful going back down the mountain."

Emma sniffed again and stalked out the door without responding. In a minute he heard the four-wheeler crank up and roar away from the cabin. He went to the door and watched her flying back down the hill, dust roiling up behind her. "I hope she'll be okay."

"I think she'll be fine. I'm more worried about anything she'd meet on the way down." Camron laughed and put an arm around Travis's waist. "Thanks for standing up to her, kit. And for telling her about us. I know it wasn't easy. I thought you were about to try to take off with her."

"I was mad earlier, but I did some thinking at the creek. This is where I want to be. With you, I mean."

"Glad to hear it." He pulled Travis into his arms and brushed his lips against his. "Because I had no intentions of letting you go, even if I had to whip both your asses."

****

Plan B

Emma was taking her time going back down the mountain. She had a lot of thinking to do and she was madder than hell. A damn MacKay as her boy's mate! She knew what Travis said was right—there wasn't a damn thing anybody could do about it, and that made her even madder. Then, there was the idea of Spencer making decisions about Travis behind her back. Had everybody suddenly gone crazy, or had she?

She'd probably been traveling for about fifteen or twenty minutes and was so lost in her thoughts that she didn't realize at first that she'd been hearing a noise like other ATVs on the trail for some time now. She pulled over to the side of the trail and listened. The hum of their engines was definitely getting closer. She moved as far off the trail as she could, partially hiding herself from view behind a large bush.

Two four-wheelers topped a little rise and she saw them. Spencer and Hawke with what looked like Hawke's mate riding with him. She stepped out onto the trail, and they skidded to a stop a few yards in front of her.

Spencer got to her first, jumping off his vehicle and running over to her. "Mama, are you okay?"

She held up a hand to halt him and raised her nose in the air. "What do you care, Spencer Sutherland? You and your brother have both turned against me. That much is painfully clear."

"What are you talking about, Mama? You know that's not true."

"Aunt Emma…"

"You hush your mouth, Hawke Sutherland," she said, turning towards him. "I'll deal with you in a minute." She turned toward Jace then. "I hope you didn't break your mama's heart when you threw in with this one." She jerked a thumb toward Hawke.

"No, ma'am. My parents threw me out several years ago when I told them I was gay."

"Well, I'm sorry for that, but at least you didn't choose *him* over your own mother." She gave Hawke an aggrieved look.

"Mama, please…just settle down and make sense."

"Sense? Does it make sense to keep secrets from me when my youngest son has the misfortune to be the mate of a MacKay? And two clan males at that, who'll probably just kill each other before this mess is over with. And my other son lied to me about it!" As Spencer started to protest, she held up an imperious hand. "A lie of omission is still a lie, young man."

Spencer flushed and looked down, unable to hold her gaze.

"I went to get Travis, and he wouldn't come with me, told me that he would come back down the mountain with Camron. Can you believe that? He chose a MacKay over his own mother."

"Mama, I doubt that Travis meant it that way. He's not choosing Camron over you. It's just that if they *are* mates, he doesn't have any choice about who to stay with. Isn't that right, Hawke?"

"Oh, Lord, Spencer, please leave me out of this."

Plan B

"Very wise of you, Hawke," Emma said. "You've done enough. Oh, I know you're in this up to your eyebrows. You and Spencer are thick as thieves and always have been. Anyway, I'm sick of all of you, and I'm going home."

"Fine. We'll ride back down with you and make sure you get home okay."

"I don't need you to ride with me."

"I know, but we're going to anyway."

She gave a final little glare at them and climbed back on her vehicle, cranking it back up and flying down the mountain past them. They were hard put to keep up with her as she raced back down the trail.

Chapter Eight

Travis wasn't sure how the fight escalated so quickly. One minute he and Camron were sitting at the table, having a cup of coffee and talking, and the next minute, they were yelling at each other. It all started when Camron reminded him again that they really needed to get back home and go to work.

"Yeah, about that. Camron, I can't let my father down. I need to keep my promise to him and work in the store in Blackwater Falls."

Camron shook his head. "No, Travis. I need you with me."

"But why? Your brother can help you out, can't he? You don't need my help."

"Yes I do. Will is going to college, and he won't be able to help out much longer. Besides, this is my business, and my mate needs to help me build it."

Travis pressed his lips together and shook his head. He had to set his foot down or Camron would try to run over him at every turn. He had one thing in common with Travis's mama whether he knew it or not—he was bull headed and wanted his own way. If he didn't get it, he pitched a fit, and Travis had no intention of fighting him on every decision for the rest of their long lives. He'd settle this thing now, or there'd never be peace between them.

"You can hire someone to help if you need it that bad. But I've already made my plans to run the store."

Plan B

"Made your plans? You were lying on your ass in the house when I came to get you—don't give me that shit! You probably think you can slack off at the store. Go in when you feel like it and take off early if you want to…hell, not even go in at all when you get the urge to tie one on with Holden and the boys!"

"Holden and the boys? How did they come into this? Hell no, I'm not thinking about all that. I'm thinking that my daddy asked me to help him out, and that's what I need to do."

"I happen to know your *daddy* has been trying to get you to work in the store for years now. I hear all the talk around town. And you haven't felt this overpowering urge to help him out before this. Why now, all of a sudden? No, Travis, I won't have you sliding back into your lazy ways. You'll do as I say."

Travis jumped to his feet and slammed a hand on the table. "You go to hell!"

"I'm already there! Damn it, I'm tired of fighting you and your whole damn family at every turn. This isn't the kind of life I envisioned for myself either, you know! All I ever wanted was a nice little girl to settle down with and have a few kids---a nice quiet, *respectable* life! Instead, look at what I got—a crazy, wild-ass boy, that I don't even like all that much!"

A silence fell down between them at the words and Camron seemed to realize what he'd said. He flushed a dark red, but his lips were in a stubborn, thin line as he stared back at Travis, and his back stayed unbending and firm.

Travis had never known words could be so hurtful before he got involved with Camron. He used them like a weapon when he wanted to, and these last words were hurled at him like little pointed barbs, sticking into his skin. They wouldn't kill him, but they wounded, just as Camron had intended them to. Travis nodded once and walked toward the door. He grabbed his jacket and cap off the hook by the door and put them on. Putting his hand on the doorknob, he hesitated. He didn't want to look back at Camron, though he could feel his gaze heavy on his back. If he looked back, he might not find the courage to walk out.

"I'm going home, Camron. We tried this thing and it didn't work. I'm not what you need, and I don't want to be some consolation prize you had to take. Like you just said, you don't even like me very much. I know this mate thing is strong, but we can find a way to stay away from each other. I'm sorry I wasted your time."

Without turning, he waited—waited a long moment to give Camron a chance to call him back, to tell him he didn't mean the things he'd said, and tell him not to go, but Camron never said a word. That was enough answer in itself. Feeling his shoulders slump, Travis walked out, closing the door quietly behind him. He stood for a moment on the front porch, unable to drag enough oxygen into his lungs. Then he walked slowly down the steps and started down the trail for home.

Plan B

Hard to believe it was over as quickly and unexpectedly as it had begun. Was it that easy for Camron to let Travis go? Was he even now sitting at the table, weak with relief that he didn't have to do this anymore? Because Travis was having a much harder time of things--it wasn't nearly so easy for him.

It would be nice if he could just turn off his brain and not keep thinking and rethinking how it had all gone wrong so fast and knowing how much he was going to miss this man he hadn't even been that aware of until a few days ago when he'd come storming into his life. He didn't want to remember the way those hazel eyes of his crinkled at the corners when he smiled, or that slow, sexy grin, or the way he smelled, like something musky and sweet and spicy all at the same time. He didn't want to think about his soft southern drawl that got so slow when they made love, or the way his voice seemed all velvety and soft when he called him *kit*.

Well, it was over now, and it was all for the best, really. A wave of tiredness washed over him, but he kept determinedly walking. It wasn't all that far down the mountain, only about five or six miles. And like everybody kept telling him over and over, he wasn't a kid anymore. He'd get over this thing with Camron, because he had to. He didn't want to be with somebody who didn't want him.

He'd been walking down the trail for about fifteen minutes when he came to the first fork. He stopped and tried to remember which way they'd come as they traveled up the mountain, but he wasn't sure. There weren't even any tracks in the rocky terrain that he could pick out from his mama's recent trip down in the ATV. Sighing, he took the right fork, figuring as long as it was going down the mountain, he'd probably be okay. Maybe he'd come across another cabin up here somewhere. If he did, he'd stop and ask to use their phone. He could call Spencer to come after him. He didn't remember passing any cabins on the way up the trail, but he'd been pretty distracted at the time and maybe hadn't noticed.

He tried not to think any more about Camron as he walked, knowing that when he did, when he allowed himself to realize it was over, it was going to be devastating. He knew, of course, that Camron had always liked women. He'd made no secret of that, but he thought he was changing his mind a little, at least about him. He knew he was a fuck-up and that he didn't have the best reputation in town, but he never dreamed that Camron didn't even like him much. That hurt maybe most of all.

He thought that Camron wanted to be with him, and that they'd been growing closer. How stupid was that? How stupid was it that he actually thought Camron would try to stop him from leaving? Just a couple of hours before he'd told him that he would never let him go and then they'd made love again. It had felt like making love to him anyway. Maybe Camron was just going through the motions.

Plan B

Up ahead he spotted a little rise with a wisp of smoke coming over the trees in the distance-- a cabin in the hills above town, then. He quickened his pace, hurrying toward it, anxious to get off this mountain now that he'd made his choice. Not that he expected Camron to come after him, even if he had spent most of the walk down looking back over his shoulder.

He'd just come within shouting distance of the cabin, and was able to make out that it was a small place, and pretty rundown when he spotted someone on the front porch. An old, battered jeep was pulled up outside too and when he saw the man on the porch raise his arm, Travis thought at first that he was waving at him. Travis lifted his own arm to wave when a puff of dirt lifted in the trail in front of him with a little popping sound. The report of the rifle came a second later as Travis realized the man had shot at him.

Stumbling backward, he fell on his ass and rolled toward the woods on the side of the trail. Something slammed into the tree next to him, just over his head, splintering the wood and raining little bits of bark and tree sap down on his cap. He scrambled to his feet, diving for deeper cover in the woods when another bullet whizzed past so close to his head that it knocked his cap off and seared a path of fire along his cheek and by his temple.

In a panic, he realized that this last bullet had come from closer by, just beyond the other side of the trail. He tried to get to his feet, but his legs didn't want to work, and blood was slipping down into his eyes. Before he could even register the pain, he fell down on his chest to rest a second—just a second before he tried to make it out of there. His last conscious thought was of Camron, and how unsurprised he'd be to know Travis had taken the wrong fork in the road and run into trouble—how once again, he'd managed to fuck everything up.

****

Camron was packing up the four-wheeler when he heard the shots and he knew without a shadow of a doubt that something had happened to Travis. There were three shots in fairly rapid succession and maybe it was instinct—maybe some kind of weird side effect of the mating call, but he knew those shots had been directed at Travis. The sure knowledge made his heart stutter in his chest before it started back with a wild thumping and caused a sick thrill of terror to flare through him.

Ruthlessly quelling his first impulse to race wildly down the mountain in the direction of the shots, he forced himself back inside to locate his hunting rifle and then attach it to the gun rack on the front of his four-wheeler. Though he hurried, he kept his movements sure and methodical, not allowing himself to fly apart like he wanted to.

Plan B

In minutes, he was hurtling down the hill, finally giving in to the overwhelming need for speed, chasing the sound of the shots still reverberating through his head. The minute Travis left, Camron knew he'd made a mistake. His words had been thoughtless and mean, and he hadn't even meant them, really. Yet there was a part of him that said, the hell with him, let him go. You don't need some crazy boy fucking your life up, changing all your plans.

The funny thing was that the second he'd heard those shots and was faced with the real possibility of losing Travis, none of those plans seemed important or even worthwhile in any way. All he could think of was getting to him and that the last words they'd spoken to each other were hurtful and cruel.

Camron had already made up his mind to follow him and catch up with him on the trail before he'd heard the shots. He knew he was only kidding himself, and he knew he couldn't stay away from Travis. He figured he'd apologize and talk him into coming home with him where he belonged.

He'd been taking his time, closing everything up to leave, and giving Travis a chance to cool off and calm down. He figured he was only twenty minutes ahead of him, and he could catch up to him easily enough. No problem. Never in a million years did he expect Travis to get himself in some kind of trouble before he could get to him. Never did he think for one minute that his time might be up.

When he got to the first fork in the trail, he almost flew right down the hill, but something told him Travis might have taken the wrong fork. He hadn't exactly been in the best shape when he'd brought him here a few days before. He needed to at least check it out. Camron circled back, making himself go slowly and look for tracks and sure enough, there on the wrong fork about ten yards down, he found a boot print sunk in the soft dirt in the middle of the trail.

Trying hard to remember what was down that trail, he could only come up with an old deserted cabin about a half a mile ahead. One of his great-uncles had lived there up until maybe seven or eight years before, when he moved his elderly wife closer to Blackwater Falls and the doctor there. As far as he knew, no one had moved back. Squatters could have taken it over, but this was all MacKay land, and he couldn't imagine anyone being dumb enough to trespass on it. Even discounting all the No Trespassing signs posted everywhere, the locals knew never to hunt or even get close to property belonging to the MacKays and the Sutherlands.

Plan B

While no one in the area suspected the true nature of the clans, there had been enough intermarriage with the locals to have a little information floating around, even though the humans they mated with eventually had to cast off all ties with at least their extended relatives, at a minimum. Once out of school, the clan members cut all ties with the humans they'd known there, because the shifters lived so much longer and aged very slowly as the years passed by. Still, enough of a mystique had grown up around Blackwater Falls and the clan that locals knew to avoid the area at all costs, and outsiders were "discouraged" from visiting.

On the chance that some squatters had taken up residence in the cabin, though, Camron headed straight for it, a feeling of sick dread urging him on. The bullet that came through his windshield as he got close to the cabin shocked the hell out of him and made him swerve onto the shoulder, spin out hard and then land the four-wheeler on its side in a ditch at the edge of the woods. He jumped and rolled out of the wreckage at the last minute, with only his supernaturally quick reflexes saving him from serious injury. Clan members joked about their "cat-like" reflexes, but it was all too true, and this time they had saved him from being crushed under the weight of the ATV.

Falling down onto his belly, Camron crawled to the shelter of the deeper forest and pulled out his hunting knife. He couldn't make it back for his rifle, because he realized that the shot had come from somewhere in the woods, and the shooter might be watching him even now. He needed the heavy comfort of the big knife in his hand.

He looked back toward the trail, trying to get a glimpse of whoever was shooting at him and spotted something pale blue lying near the ditch where he'd wrecked his ATV. Peering closer, he saw that it was a baseball cap, turned up on its side. A dark bloodstain spread out over the side of it, and the knowledge that it was Travis's cap punched into him like a fist. His stomach threatened to empty itself in a sick panic.

Two more bullets thunked into the tree just above his head. He yelled like he'd been hit and flattened himself in the grass. His hand clutched the knife beneath him as he waited. Playing possum was the oldest trick in the book. When he was a kid he'd done it with his friends during their war games all the time, and it even worked sometimes. Probably that was why it was such an old trick—because people still occasionally fell for it.

After a long silence, he finally heard footsteps coming toward him. Heart hammering, he lay as still as he possibly could, not even daring to breathe. He was taking a chance that the guy wouldn't shoot him again to make sure he was really dead, or at least not too soon. His luck held steady, and when the footsteps were right beside him, he heard a click as the shooter cocked his piece ready to deliver the killing shot. Springing to his feet, he buried the knife in the man's stomach, twisting the blade and watching his face as his eyes widened in shock and blood bubbled at his lips.

Plan B

Afterward, he stood over the body, looking down at him for a long time, watching the man's eyes glaze over and stare frozenly up at the sky. He knew he should feel pity or remorse for what he'd done, but it was hard to feel either one. The man had tried his best to kill Camron and may have killed--no, he wouldn't allow himself to think of that. Travis may have been wounded, but he *wasn't* dead. He couldn't be. He'd know it if he was.

And if he was wrong and this son-of-a-bitch had killed Travis, he'd try his best to revive him, so he could kill him all over again.

He gazed down at the man lying on the side of the trail and realized he'd never seen him before. He was about sixty, with a scruffy beard and wearing a dirty camo jacket, jeans and cheap hunting boots. He looked like any number of older men you might see on any day at the Walmart around this part of the world, though maybe a little more disreputable than most.

He had just bent down to go through his pockets when he heard the sound of four-wheelers coming toward him. Camron ducked quickly back into the woods and hid himself behind a big pine near the forest's edge, wishing like hell he'd had a chance to get his gun off the rack. As the sound drew nearer, he realized that it was two ATVs, coming fast, and he sagged with relief as he peered around the tree and saw that it was Hawke and Spencer, both of them with rifles secured to the racks of their machines.

He watched as they skidded to a stop by the dead man on the side of the trail, and Camron saw Hawke jump off and kneel beside the man Camron had killed. Hawke's young mate, sitting on the back of one of the vehicles, looked shocked and scared. As Camron stepped out of the woods, Hawke stood up quickly, jumping in front of his mate, his eyes widening when he recognized Camron.

"Goddammit, Camron, what's happened here?" Hawke gestured toward him. "Is any of that blood yours?"

Camron glanced down at himself. His entire shirt front and both forearms were covered in gore, but he shook his head grimly and gestured toward the dead man. "No, it's all his."
Spencer came around the side of his vehicle and gripped Camron's shoulder. "What about Travis?" he said urgently, shaking him a little. "Camron, where's my brother?"

****

It had taken about an hour to get Emma safely down the mountain and extricate themselves from her. Hawke resisted at first when Spencer insisted they go back up and make sure that Travis was okay.

"C'mon, Spencer, haven't they been bothered enough? According to your mother, Travis was fine but still refused to come back with her. Leave them alone!"

"I don't want to bother them, Hawke. But we both know what kind of guilt trip my mama can lay on you—hell, I'm feeling the effects myself!"

Plan B

"So? Travis can handle it too if you give him the chance. He has Camron to help him now."

Spencer got that mulish expression that his whole family was prone to. "Damn it, Hawke, I'm going up there with or without you."

Hawke felt Jace touch him warningly on the back and he shook his head and sighed. "All right, we'll go with you. But we won't stay and bother them once you've satisfied yourself he's okay—got it?"

"Got it," Spencer said, grinning. Spencer had been doing this to him since they were kids and had gotten him into a lot of trouble this way over the years. Still, it was fairly early in the day, and he'd promised Jace a ride up the mountain. He turned his four-wheeler around and followed Spencer back up the trail.

It was only about fifteen minutes later that they heard the gunshots. Hawke stopped first and Spencer pulled up beside him. "Did you hear that?"

"Yeah, I did. Do you think that it's hunters?"

"Shouldn't be—not around here. Could be poachers, I guess. Let's make sure that Travis and Camron are okay."

Ten minutes later, they were just past the last fork in the trail on the way to Camron's cabin when they heard another series of shot coming from down the opposite fork. Hawke and Spencer both stopped and glanced over at each other. Hawke turned to Jace. "Get off, baby, and wait for me while I go check this out."

"Hell, no," Jace said, tightening his grip around Hawke's waist.

"Jace," he said, making his voice deeper and more stern. "I don't have time to play around. Now get off and wait for me by the side of the trail. I'll be back in a few minutes, but if I'm not for some reason, start walking back down the mountain, and I'll catch up with you."

"Don't use that sheriff voice with me, and I'm not going anywhere but down that trail with you. If you think I am, you've got another think coming." Jace glared back at him belligerently, and Hawke blew out an irritated breath.

"Jace…

"No, damn it. Now get on down there and see what it is. I'll stay out of your way, but I'm not going to hide on the side of the trail, so you can forget that shit."

Hawke huffed out his exasperation, but Spencer yelled over at him. "Damn it, Hawke, stop trying to be Papa Bear and let him come with us. We need to see what that is!"

Hawke pointed a finger at Jace. "You stay low behind me, you hear? And if anything happens, you stay the hell out of it!"

"Okay, okay, let's go." Jace pushed his finger away and gave him a cheeky wink. "You're not half as scary as you think you are."

Plan B

Hawke gave him a look of affronted outrage and turned back around to follow Spencer who was already taking off down the trail. Hawke's more powerful vehicle caught up with him in a minute or two, and as they rounded the first bend in the trail they both must have seen the overturned four-wheeler lying on its side in the ditch at the same time. A body was lying flat on its back beside it, its arms outstretched onto the trail.

Hawke had a bad moment when he recognized Camron's four-wheeler, but by the time he'd stopped and jumped off beside the body, he'd already realized it wasn't Camron or Travis. This man was older and heavier. He had time to register the fact that the man was not only dead, but that he had a huge, bloody stab wound in the stomach, when a movement caught his eye, and he whirled around and managed to get in front of Jace in time to see Camron, covered in blood, stepping from the cover of the trees.

"Goddammit, Camron, what's happened here?" Hawke's gestured toward Camron's shirtfront. "Is any of that blood yours?"

Camron glanced down at himself, then gestured toward the dead man. "No, it's all his." He seemed shocked and traumatized, despite the coolness of his tone, but before Hawke could make him sit down, Spencer lunged around the side of his vehicle and gripped Camron's shoulder. "What about Travis?" he said urgently, shaking him a little. "Camron, where's my brother?"

Camron shook his head, his eyes haunted. "I-I don't know. I was coming for him when…"

Hawke pushed Spencer off him and helped him to sit down on the side of the trail. "Tell us, Camron. Where's Travis?"

"We-we had an argument after his mother left. Just something stupid, but we both got mad and said stupid shit. Travis said he was leaving and started back down the trail." He lifted anguished eyes to Hawke. "I was coming after him, but I was giving him time to cool off—you know how he is—and then I heard the shots. I knew it was him. I knew he was in trouble."

Spencer made a noise beside him, but Hawke kept his focus on Camron. "Take your time, Camron. Just tell us."

"I could tell the shots were coming from down here, so I was coming for him when that guy," he jerked a thumb over at the body, "shot at me from the bushes. I wrecked my four-wheeler and then I played dead when he shot at me again. I waited till he got close and…" He held up the bloody hunting knife. "I used this on him and I-I killed him." He scrambled to his feet, knocking away their hands. "I got to get to Travis. I think he's been shot."

"What?" Spencer yelled, grabbing his shoulder and whirling him around. "What are you saying?"

Camron pointed toward a blue hat on the ground. "T-That's his hat. He was wearing it when he left."

They all looked at the blood stain on the side of the cap at the same time, and a shocked little silence fell among them. Camron broke it when he cried out. "He's *not* dead. He's not! I'd feel it if he was, Hawke. You know I would!"

Hawke nodded. "Yes, I believe you would, Camron. Just calm down and let me think a minute."

Plan B

"Hawke!" Spencer cried out beside him, running a hand distractedly through his hair, his eyes filling with tears. His anxiety was doubled in Camron—Hawke thought for sure he'd jump out of his skin any second.

"Calm down, both of you!" Jace's soft, but urgent tone cut through the tension, and made them all turn toward him. "This isn't going to help Travis one damn bit. Now think about it! There has to be more than one of them. Somebody took Travis." Jace gestured over to a set of boot tracks leading off the trail. Beside the tracks, there was evidence that someone had dragged something heavy off onto a small track that led up toward the cabin on the hill above.

"It could have been his body," Spencer said, his voice hoarse and half-choked.

"No!" Camron shook his head firmly. "He's not dead—maybe hurt, but not dead." He headed off toward his ATV to get his gun. "I'm going after him!"

"We'll all go, but let's not charge up the hill like Chuck Norris, damn it. Camron, you and Spencer get off in the woods and head up around the back. Get above it if you can, and I'll go up through the woods to the front of the cabin." Hawke reached down to pull a revolver from an ankle holster. "Jace, keep this just in case. You're with me."

Camron started off but Hawke pulled him around to face him. "Camron, don't do anything stupid, and give me a chance to get in place. I'll try to draw their attention."

He nodded curtly and took off, with Spencer right behind him. "It'll take them a minute to get in place. That will give us time to get up the hill, since I have to move slower with you."

Jace nodded, and Hawke knew he realized he wasn't being condescending. The cougar shifters had phenomenal speed when they needed it even in their human forms—at least for short bursts of time. Camron and Spencer were probably already halfway up the hill by this time. "Please stay behind me, baby, and don't take any chances."

Jace nodded again, touching his arm reassuringly, perhaps realizing Hawke had to keep warning him to be cautious—the idea of what might have happened to Travis was riding him hard. He'd been the one to urge Spencer to back off when Camron wanted to bring Travis up here, and even though none of this was Camron's fault, they all knew how volatile a love match between two clan males could be. Hawke was feeling guilty that he hadn't insisted they stay closer to town until they worked out their relationship.

Hawke got his rifle, along with some extra ammunition he always kept in his packs on the ATV and filled his pockets with it. Then with a nod to Jace to follow him, he took off up the hill toward the cabin.

****

Plan B

When the kick landed in his ribs, Travis jerked awake. Before he could move, a single-barreled shotgun jammed against his forehead. He pulled back violently, which was a stupid move, because it caused pain to come crashing down on him, so bad he had to grit his teeth to keep from biting his damn tongue off. The pain seemed to emanate from the side of his head, and he remembered suddenly the bullet blazing its way along his cheek. He was sick at his stomach and had to swallow down the nausea that threatened to make him vomit all over the boots of the shotgun owner.

Managing to get his eyes fully open, he squinted up at the man, who kept the gun pressed firmly to his forehead. "Who the fuck are you, boy?"

The words were spit at him by the guy holding the gun, a man a little older than he was, and probably thirty or forty pounds heavier. He was dressed like a hunter in filthy camo, and he stunk like cigarettes and beer with a heavy dose of pot. The whole place reeked of it, as a matter of fact.

Travis straightened up carefully, not wanting to jar his wound and start a fresh torrent of pain. Any more of that and he definitely would throw up his breakfast.

"I said, who the fuck are you?"

"Travis Sutherland," he managed to get out, his voice sounding rusty and hoarse. "Who the fuck are you?"

The man grinned down at him and slowly pumped the action of his shotgun. "Don't try me, boy. A Sutherland, huh? What the hell you doin' up here on MacKay land?"

Deciding not to poke the bear any more than he had to, Travis answered him. "I came up here to go fishing. I've been staying at my friend's cabin."

"So it's your wood smoke we been seein' and smellin' for the past few days. And just where is this friend of yours?"

"He left early this morning," Travis lied. "I was hiking down after him and took the wrong fork in the road."

"Hiking?" The man snorted with contempt. "If that's true, you're an unlucky motherfucker, I'll tell you that, 'cause you done took a hell of a wrong trail. Is anybody else up here with you?"

Travis bit his lip, unsure of the right answer. If he said no, then that might keep Camron safe, giving him a chance to leave his cabin and get on down the mountain. But if he stalled for time and said yes, they might not be so quick to kill Travis and dispose of his body in the woods. Maybe Camron would check on him and find out he hadn't gone home and tell Hawke. Another nudge of the gun encouraged him to come up with quicker answer.

"No, but some other friends are on their way up. One of them is the sheriff, Hawke Sutherland. He's my cousin."

"Damn it!" Someone from behind Camo said. "I told you not to shoot at him! Damn Hawke Sutherland's a mean-ass son-of-a-bitch! If we kill his kin, he ain't never gonna let it go!"

Another man paced restlessly forward and squatted down beside Travis. He was older than the other one with a grizzled growth of gray beard on his face and chewing tobacco stains on the sides of his mouth. He leaned over close enough for Travis to smell the stink of his rotting teeth.

Plan B

"How soon is he comin', boy? Does he know we're here?"

Travis shrugged. "I don't know when he's coming. Soon, I think. And I didn't know you were here, so I doubt he does. Just let me go, and I won't say anything."

"Bullshit!' Camo sneered. He turned to the man with the gray beard before jerking up his gun. "I say shoot him and bury him in the woods."

"And then what, stupid? You think they won't be looking for him?"

A series of three shots—one, and then two more close together--sounded from behind them, and they jumped away and ran for the door. Travis tried to get to his feet, but he was dizzy and shaky. His eyes quickly scanned the room, and he found that he was in an old cabin, even smaller and way dirtier than Camron's. It stunk of old grease and wood smoke, with the sickly sweet odor of pot so strong it hung in the air around them like a curtain. A single, bare window let in weak sunlight over his head and another window was by the open door. Through this door, he could see the two men leaning over the porch rail and gesturing wildly down toward what must be the road. They were having an urgent discussion about somebody named Tim, and wondering what the hell he was shooting at now. As the silence stretched out, they got more and more nervous. Camo-man wanted to go down and check on him, but the other man held him back, whispering something and jerking his head toward Travis. Both men seemed strung out and nervous, a bad combination with a loaded shot gun in hand.

The roar of ATVs sounded from the road below and the effect on the two men would have been funny in any other situation. They began to wave their arms around, and the older man actually threw down his cap and pulled at his hair.

Camo was probably the most dangerous. He was burly and fat, but Travis figured he'd be able to take him down. Even wounded, his strength was much greater than either of the humans. Given his current condition, Travis doubted his ability to get them both, and that shotgun was already primed and pumped. Still, he was going to try it. No way was he going to sit there and let them shoot him. They were becoming more and more agitated and Travis knew one or the other was about to snap. He had to do something and quick if they came back in that door for him or started shooting down the hill.

Because if there was any chance those shots might be directed somehow at Camron…that didn't bear thinking about. He readied himself to act, managing to get to his knees and getting ready to spring on Camo-man when he walked back through the door. With any luck, he could easily put him out of commission before he got the gun back up.

A sudden loud shout from outside startled him almost as badly as it did the men on the porch. It came from close by and it sounded like Hawke!

"You there on the porch! Throw down your guns and put your hands in the air! This is the Sheriff, and we have you surrounded!"

Plan B

As if on cue, two more shots fired, this time from the back of the cabin, one on the left and one on the right. It seemed as if they really were surrounded, and for the first time, Travis felt a bit of hope.

The two men scrambled back from the porch, cussing and yelling and Camo came straight for him, the gun stuck out in front of him. "Git on your feet, boy."

He jerked Travis up before he could react and dragged him to the front door, the barrel of the shotgun stuck in the side of his neck. Dizzy and sick, Travis didn't try to fight him, just biding his time to see what Hawke had up his sleeve. Camo obviously planned to use him as a bargaining chip, so he let himself be hauled over to the door.

Camo kept the gun tightly wedged against his neck. "Here's one of your men, sheriff! I'll blow his head off if any of you come any closer!"

"You shoot him and you're a dead man! Let him go and it'll go easier on you!"

"You're a sheriff! You can't shoot us down in cold blood."

"You shoot that boy, and you can just fuckin' watch me, asshole! Let him go and throw down your damn guns!"

"Hell no! Let us get to our ATV and get out of here. We'll put him out unharmed by the end of the road."

Graybeard plucked nervously at Camo-man's jacket. "Let him go, Earl. We're caught. Ain't no sense in makin' things any worse than they are."

Travis spoke up, surprised at how weak his voice sounded. "Listen to your friend, Earl. The sheriff will kill you if you don't throw down your gun."

"Shut the hell up!" Earl hit Travis with a solid blow to the injured side of his face, and the pain exploded with a bright burst in his head. He cried out helplessly, and all hell suddenly broke loose.

Something seemed to literally fly across the porch and rip him out of Camo's arms while a shot gun blast sounded so close to his ears that he was deafened by it for a minute or two. Everything around him seemed to go in slow, soundless motion as he was pushed firmly down to his knees and watched Earl's body hurtling across the rail, with another body—he thought it might be Spencer's, diving after it. Somebody hunched over him then, cutting off his view, but he could smell the comforting fragrance of Camron's body, and he relaxed instantly, his hands going up to clutch at Camron's shirt and pull him closer. Finally able to relax, he let the muted noise of the battle drift over him. The pain faded a little as he felt the brush of Camron's lips on his cheek, and his arms were strong and comforting around him.

Chapter Nine

Travis lay back on the pillows in Camron's bed and wished everybody would just go away. The small bedroom was crowded with people, and if it weren't for Camron sitting beside him, holding tightly to his hand, he would have jumped up and left, leaving them to fight it out amongst themselves.

For the past ten minutes, his mama had been trying to convince Camron that Travis needed to come back home with her—just for a few days—but he just kept calmly shaking his head. He was surprised at how placidly Camron was taking her continued insistence. As a matter of fact he'd been uncharacteristically quiet since they arrived back at his house. He'd called for the doctor who'd examined Travis, while Camron stood by the bed and held his hand.

Travis wondered if he was still bothered by what he'd had to do earlier to the man on the trail. He hadn't known about it until Hawke and Spencer came in talking about it. Camron hadn't talked about it at all and changed the subject when Travis brought it up.

Travis's mama was still talking about taking him home while he listened with only half an ear when his dad suddenly spoke up, surprising everybody in the room. "Emma, that's enough," he said quietly. "Now you've seen Travis, and he's in good hands here with his mate." He took her firmly by the arm and began to lead her from the room. "Travis is fine and Camron's got everything under control, so we'll be leaving."

She sputtered a bit, but took one long look at his face and nodded. "Camron, you take care of my baby, and I'll come back…" A little squeeze of her arm and she winced as she amended her words. "I'll call you tomorrow."

She gave Travis a little wave and allowed her husband to pull her out of the room, giving Hawke and Spencer a look that blistered their faces and should have peeled the paint off the walls behind them as she passed them near the door. Hawke averted his gaze, and Spencer flinched, as Jace and Travis looked at each other and laughed out loud.

"My big, strong sheriff," Jace said. "He'll go up against a man armed with a shotgun any day, but can't even look at one of the clan females when she's pissed off."

"A man with a shotgun isn't half as scary and talks a lot less," Spencer muttered.

"*Anyway,*" Hawke said, shooting Jace a dirty look before looking back at Travis, "we came to see how you were and tell you about what we found out after you left this afternoon."

"Oh yeah," Camron said. "All I could think about was getting Travis down the mountain and over to the doctor's office. I sort of left you and Spencer to clean up the mess, didn't I?" He grinned up at them ruefully and tightened his hold on Travis's wrist.

Travis smiled at him. "I told you I was okay—the bullet only grazed me. I lost a little blood, that's all."

"A little blood? I thought somebody had been killing hogs in that room!"

"Well, head wounds bleed a lot. I was okay."

"I don't blame him for being scared, Travis," Spencer said. "When that dude brought you out on the porch you were as white as a sheet and pouring blood down your face. And then when that bastard hit you, I didn't think anyone could move any quicker to get to you than I could, but Camron beat me by a mile."

Camron flushed a little and shrugged. "It pissed me off. I didn't like seeing him that way."

"You think?" Spencer chuckled. "I told you the man who hit him was already dead from the fall off the porch, and you still punched him in the face."

Camron shrugged and looked ashamed. "Not my finest moment."

Spencer smiled. "I don't know--I kind of liked it."

"You're both bloodthirsty," Jace said. "The other man surrendered without a fight, didn't he, Hawke?"

"Yes. They were growing marijuana up behind the house, near the tree line. We got sixty- some plants from up in there. They were small-time meth cooks, too. They were doing the 'shake and bake' method and then using the pot to bring them down off the tweaks. That's one reason they were so paranoid and crazy, along with probably a natural disposition toward it." Spencer snorted beside him, and Hawke gave him a disapproving glance. "Everything's been turned over to DEA, including the prisoner."

"What were they doing up there, Hawke?" Travis asked. "I mean, were they squatters?"

"No, not exactly. The one Camron killed on the road—the one who shot you, Travis, was some sort of a MacKay by marriage. A human. He was a stepson of Camron's great-uncle. He moved away from here years ago, but when he drifted back to Huntsville, he was looking for a place to stay. He contacted his mother, and she gave him permission to stay up in the old cabin for a few months until he could get back on his feet. Of course she didn't have any idea that would involve the growing and selling of marijuana."

Camron nodded. "Good place for it—it's pretty remote."

"According to the one who gave himself up, they had been seeing the smoke from your fire for a few days but were lying low and hoping no one came around. They were paranoid as hell, and when Travis walked down that road, MacKay panicked. He was down on the road scouting around when you came up. The shot from the porch was just to scare you away, but MacKay must have panicked and shot Travis without thinking. He called to the others for help, and they came down and took you up to the cabin while he waited in case anybody else showed up."

"And that's where I came in," Camron said.

"Yes, unfortunately for him," Hawke said. "And you know the rest of the story. I explained to the agents that came how the man on the road attacked you first, and they could see the evidence with their own eyes. His rifle was cocked, and they could see you killed him in self-defense. The other one fell from the front porch in the fight. Broke his neck."

"I didn't mean to knock him over the railing, but after his gun went off next to you, he turned it on me. I had to put him out of commission, or he'd have shot me point blank."

"Live by the sword, die by it too," Jace said. "Those men tried to kill Camron and Travis. They would have killed you too Spencer."

"Anyway," Hawke said, "there won't be any trouble about it. They'll want to talk to you both, but it's just a formality. All three of them had records for violent crimes as long as my arm."

Hawke came over to put an arm around Jace. "We'll get out of here and let you guys rest for now. I'll come over in the morning to get your sworn statements."

Camron stood up to shake his hand. "Thanks for everything, Hawke. "I don't know what would have happened if you all hadn't come along."

"I still think you'd have kicked all their asses," Spencer said, slapping him on the back. "Little brother, you got yourself a good one here."

"I know," Travis said softly, smiling over at Camron, who still didn't meet his gaze.

They all left, with assurances to come by later, leaving Travis alone with Camron at last. Camron came back over immediately to sit down beside Travis again and take hold of his hand.

Travis smiled. "I'm not going anywhere, you know. You don't have to keep holding onto me."

"Damn right you're not going anywhere." Camron gave him a stern look before bringing his hand up to his lips to kiss the back of it. "You scared the hell out of me."

"I'm sorry."

"No, I'm the one who should be sorry. When I saw your cap on the road and thought you'd been shot…and then that bastard dragged you out on the porch. You were bleeding all over the place and then he hit you…I thought I'd go crazy before I got to you." His voice choked on the words, and he squeezed Travis's hand so hard it hurt. "I should never have said what I did. I didn't mean it—you have to believe me."

"I do. We both said things."

He shook his head. "No, I was worse. Look, if you want to work for your father, then I'll find somebody else to help me. We can work it out, kit. Just don't ever run off like that again."

"I won't. From now on, I'll stay and fight it out, but only on one condition."

"Which is?"

"That we get to make up like we did on the trail that first day you took me to the cabin."

"I think that most definitely can be arranged." He took Travis in his arms, and they didn't do any more talking for a long time.

The End

About the Authors

Shannon West currently lives in the South with her husband and family. A lover and avid reader of M/M romances, she began writing them a few years ago and now has over forty short stories, novellas, and novels to her credit. She was a finalist in the Rainbow Awards for 2013 and very honored to be an All Romance Ebooks Top Ten Author for 2013. She loves men and everything about them, and believes that love is love, no matter the gender. She mostly spends her days at the keyboard, trying to elude housework, which stalks her relentlessly.

You can learn more about Shannon and her books on Facebook and at her website, www.shannonwestbooks.com

Susan E Scott lives with her husband in a small town in north Georgia. They're both owned by their Yorkie, Sophie, who is the undisputed queen of the household. Susan enjoys scrapbooking, traveling and reading and writing romance. Susan writes M/F and M/M erotic romance.

Dark Hollows Press

Dark Hollows Press is a publisher of all genres of erotic expression. We believe our authors are artists and their talent shouldn't be censored, so our authors present high quality stories full of romance, desire and sometimes graphic moments that are both entertaining and erotic. We have an exclusive group of talented writers and we publish stories that range from historical to fantasy, sci-fi to contemporary.

We invite you to visit us at www.darkhollowspress.com.

Made in the USA
Charleston, SC
06 June 2014